NAMELESS

A story of faith

TAMMY LEIGH ROBINSON

Second Edition: ISBN 978-0-9958264-4-1
First Edition: ISBN 978-0-9958264-0-3
eBook ISBN 978-0-9958264-1-0
Cataloguing in Publication information available from Library and Archives Canada

Second edition Copyright©2021 Tammy Leigh Robinson
TLR Publishing, Nackawic NB Canada
First Edition Copyright©2017
Published and printed in Canada

Cover art by Sharie Hall
Cover photo by Julie Boozan
Author photo by Jodi Martin

Visit www.TammyRobinsonAuthor.com

NAMELESS is a truly inspired work that masterfully tells a story with a whole new dimension that will stretch your imagination to believe in the unseen. Hope and Faith are not only characteristics of the main heroine, but personified creatively by the author. Life is a battle, and this book draws the curtain back to unveil the forces of what we do not see.

Thanh Campbell
Author, *Orphan 32*
www.Orphan32.com

An amazing book -both inspiring and informative. Tammy Robinson has skillfully woven historical facts and biblical truths with fiction to create an intriguing novel you won't want to put down. Her story-telling expertise makes this book both thought-provoking and entertaining. You will lose yourself in its pages while perhaps re-evaluating your own personal belief systems.

Sue Augustine
Best-selling author, *When Your Past is Hurting Your Present*
www.SueAugustine.com

I have an appreciation for all religions and faiths. The theme of this story transcends across all religions. It relates to the inner conflicts we all face and the power it takes to overcome the harshest of circumstances. I can relate wholeheartedly with the main character's journey to discovering faith and overcoming illness. This truly was a remarkable story.

Empowerment Coach
Best-selling Co-author, *Journeys to Success 2*
www.AmyThomson.ca

To my late daughter, Wendy Martina May Fraser.

The six months and eleven days that I had you in my life

were one of the greatest blessings I've ever had. Loving you,

and having to say good-bye too soon, has given me the

courage to face challenges with strength and confidence.

One day we will be together again. Until then, have fun

playing with the lions and the lambs in heaven,

and rolling down the grassy hills.

I love you!

Foreword

This is a beautiful, yet heart-wrenching story that compels you to read to the very end. You first meet a thirteen-year-old girl raised in a traditional Jewish home whose life drastically changes from a very happy one to isolation and shame. With a family that continues to love her and care for her from afar she lives alone for a little over a decade. Then she is told she only has a few days or weeks to live and suddenly, with death hanging over her she starts to truly live.

After hearing that an Amazing Healer has come to her neighbouring town, she is surrounded by Light and Dark Angels. They battle for her soul taking her through extremes of Hope and Doubt; Peace and Fear; Strength and Weakness; Life and Death whether she stays put or ventures out, is caught and stoned. Faith gives her the final courage to go to this man they are calling the Messiah. If she can just reach Him… If she can just touch "the tassels that dangled in front of her"… life would begin anew.

In this book we revisit a familiar time and place we have carried forward for centuries and meet one of the nameless many who was healed by having and holding close a strong FAITH in the power of LOVE.

CAROLYN SHANNON,
Women of Worth Magazine

Acknowledgements

First and foremost, I thank my Heavenly Father for giving me this story. One Sunday in 1997, He told me that the next day He would give me a story to write. He did. He's given me every word you read within these pages. I, however, let life get in the way, and put the story on the shelf many times. God has never given up on me. He continued to remind me of the story He put within me. He's never given up on you, either. That is one reason He kept encouraging me to write this book. He wants YOU to know that you can reach your goals, whatever they are.

I also want to thank my amazing husband, Keith. Nobody has ever loved me like Keith does. He continues to support me in everything I do. He may not be "perfect," but he is perfect for me.

Thank you Mom and Dad, Joan and Raymond Leigh. Without you, I wouldn't be here — literally! Thank you for believing in me and instilling in me the desire to do things to the best of my ability. Thank you for continually reminding me to "plan your work and work your plan." Thank you for supporting me in fulfilling my dream of publishing this book.

To my amazing children, thank you! Steve, you did an amazing job on my website. I don't know anyone as intelligent as you. I'm amazed that you are my son! Julie, thank you for taking the photo of the painting for the cover of this book. You are the sweetest person I know. Your love knows no bounds. Lindy, you are the most beautiful young woman on the planet – both inside and out! I am blessed beyond measure to have each one of you in my life.

Thank you to my amazing daughter-in-law Danielle, son-in-law Chad and son-in-law Matt. I'm so thankful that you are each part of our family. Thank you for loving your spouse and bringing them so much joy!
Thank you to my awesome mother-in-law, Phyllis Robinson. You are the most supportive person I know. Thank you for accepting me into your family and loving me like your own daughter. You are truly a saint in my eyes.

To my long time BFF, Tracy Blodgett. Remember the days when we'd chat on the phone for hours and we dreamed of the future? We said someday we would look back on all the troubles we were going through and be grateful because they made us stronger women. You are the strongest woman I know! Thank you for making me a better person for knowing you and loving you.

To my friends Thanh Campbell, Amy Thomson, and Sue Augustine, thank you for reading my manuscript and writing an endorsement. I respect each one of you for the talents and gifts within you.

To my dear friend, Sharie Hall, thank you for the beautiful painting you did for the cover of this book. I had a vague idea of what I wanted and you put it on paper far better than I had ever hoped for! You are so talented!

To my friends in my W.I.L.L. group, Sonya, Sherri, Julie, Jennifer, Julie S, Jennifer, Julie B, Kimberley, Barbara, Emilie and Tracey, thank you for listening to me and loving me for who I am. You spur me on to be the best version of myself.

Thank you to Anne Day, Linda Sztanko and the others at Company of Women for the great networking, teaching and the inspiration to get it done.

To the team at TriMatrix Management Consulting Inc., thank you for your patience and guidance through the process of publishing this book. I couldn't have done it without you!

To Alexandra, my editor, thank you for your encouraging feedback. I had no idea if my writing was any good, and you gave me the confidence that I actually am a solid writer.

To my many friends and family who have loved me and supported me over the years, thank you. Each one of you has made a positive impact on my life.

To the people that have hurt me, thank you. I wouldn't be the strong woman of courage if you didn't put me through the difficult times.

And finally, to you that are reading these words… thank you for having a part in making my lifelong dream come true. I've wanted to be a writer since I was in Grade 1. I still have my stories that I wrote from that year. I hope the story that I share on these pages will inspire you to make your dreams come true! You can do it!

Table of Contents

Introduction

Many of us know several Bible stories by heart, but we often don't take the time to consider them in depth. What were the experiences really like for the people involved? What risks did they take? What was everyday life like for them? What were the customs during their time?

There are very few verses in the New Testament to tell us the story of one particular woman. She had such great faith that almost everyone knows her story, yet we don't even know her name. We all know about her, but do we *know* her? She remains *Nameless*.

For the sake of this book, I've created a name for her. I combined one of the Hebrew words for "faith" (*emuna*) and one of the Greek words for "belief" (*pistis*) and came up with "Erstis." She is the "Nameless" Woman of Faith.

During the time Jesus walked the earth, He was known as "Yeshua." The Jews had several different names for God: Yahweh, Jehovah, Eloheem, Jehovah Rapha, etc. Out of respect for God, when spelling the word, they left the out "o" — so it looked like "G-d." I have respected that tradition in this book. I have also capitalized "He" and "Him" in reverence for His deity.

As you read through this historically inspired novel, I hope that the life of the "Nameless" Woman of Faith will come alive for you, as it did for me. My prayer is that her story will inspire you to step out in faith, too.

CHAPTER ONE

The Poor Rich Sick Woman

The door closed behind the doctor as he left the tiny hut. To Erstis, the sound of the latch seemed to represent the finality of a death sentence. His voice still rang in her ears, "I'm so sorry, Erstis, but there is nothing more that can be done. Your condition is worsening every day. You don't have much longer to live."

She felt as though the room was whirling about her. Her stomach churned. A knot of pain twisted inside her. She heaved, but nothing came up. Then, she lunged for the slop bucket in the corner. After several more dry heaves, the acrid taste of bile slithered up her throat. She spat into the bucket as she gasped for breath between gut-wrenching heaves.

After several minutes, the heaving began to subside. It dawned on her that she was so withered she couldn't even vomit. She slid to the floor in exhaustion, still panting. With every breath came piercing pain under her ribs, as if she had been stabbed into her, then the blade was being twisted round and round. As she lay on the floor next to the bucket, with the pungent taste of vomit in her mouth, she fought the urge to allow her eyes to close into unconsciousness.

She knew she must get up. She had to wash her face and rinse her mouth, but these days even the smallest movements seemed to drain her of energy. She moved one arm a handbreadth to her right to stabilize herself. Then, she took another deep breath as she moved her legs, which had begun to feel numb.

As she pushed herself into a sitting position, she felt as though the room was beginning to spin again. Twice she inhaled deeply, trying to fill her lungs in spite of the wrenching pain. The room reeled about her head for some time, before it began to slow down. Finally, her head stopped spinning. She set her mouth firmly in determination, and laboured up to her feet. Breathing in through her nose and exhaling through her mouth, she groped the wall for support. One painful step at a time, she made her way to the wash basin.

"I used to dance," she sighed. "Now, I stagger."

She splashed cold water on her face. Slowly, the room seemed to come back into focus. She looked up at the shelf that held her mug. Several years ago, she was able to reach up to the shelf effortlessly. Now, she had to breathe deeply and will the strength into her arm, just to lift her hand above her head in order to grasp what she needed.

She tapped her fingers on the shelf as she felt for the mug. Oh! There it is! Weakly, she grasped the mug.

The water barrel was only two steps away. It shouldn't have been a problem to walk over to it, bend down, and scoop up the water; but for Erstis, the task required a major effort. Each step required focus and determination when each of her legs felt as if it weighed as much as a cor of stones.[1] She wondered why she should even continue to push herself to drink. She knew she was going to die soon. Why should she even get out of bed? She could simply lie there in relative comfort and wither away until death took over her frail body. Surely it wouldn't take long.

When she finally reached the barrel, she placed one hand on the rim as she dipped the mug into the water. As she lifted out the filled mug, it weighed heavy in her hand. She brought her other hand up to hold the mug with both hands, as a child would do.

She lifted the mug to her parched lips and filled her mouth with the tepid water. She swished the water around in her mouth before leaning over to spit it out into the slop bucket.

After a few more deep breaths, she was finally able to ladle out a mug of milk from the large clay jar that kept it cool. She stirred in some powder made from a mixture of finely-ground herbs — a remedy that the doctor had recommended as a way to fortify the milk. "Will I never taste solid food again?" she asked aloud in an angry voice.

She gasped, closed her eyes in thought for a moment, before raising her head to gaze heavenward. "Forgive me, Father. I just miss the taste of good food.

Carrying the insipid mixture in her mug, she staggered to her cushion and sat down to sip the drink. She began to reminisce about the day her sister Hannah was married, and she especially thought of the succulent taste of roasted ewe. *Mmmm... the delicious aroma was wafting through the evening air.* She recalled the sounds of dancing and merry-making drifting across the field. Curious friends and neighbours had stolen glances at her little hut in the back field of her parents' lot. From afar, she had felt their pity – or was it judgement? Surely they thought that either she or her parents must have committed some dreadful sin, for her to be struck with such an illness. Quiet comments had circulated among the guests at the celebration.

"Erstis is the firstborn. She should have been the first one to wed."

"Unless she gets better, she'll never wed or bear children."

"The doctors say she will never be well again."

"It has been years since she became ill."

"I wonder what she did to deserve that disease."

Little did the guests know, but Erstis had a party of her own. She remembered being inside her little hut, listening to the music and even dancing a little. At the time, she wondered if her friends could hear her sing.

"Oh, I love those songs!" she sighed aloud.

That was in the early days, when she was still experimenting with remedies for her illness. Later that night, her Papa had brought her a plate of delicious food, but she barely ate any of it — and

6

what she did eat was thrown up only minutes later. That was the last time she had eaten solid food.

Shaking her head gently, as if to erase the memory, she pushed herself up off the cushion. She knew she needed to get some fresh air. Slowly, she made her way through the door and into her back yard. The small hut was at the base of a mountain cliff. When she was younger, she had enjoyed climbing up the rocky hillside.

Looking toward the fig trees, she took a deep breath, set her mouth, and forced one foot ahead of the next, but the trees seemed very far away. *I know it will be worth the effort when I can relax in the shade of the trees.* Her steps were slow as she stumbled toward her goal.

When at last she reached the shady spot, she found the cushion that was always left there for her to sit on.

"There you are, my friend," she said to the cushion. Panting, she collapsed down onto it with a thud. Closing her eyes, she took a few moments to catch her breath.

"And, you Miss Te'enah,"[2] she said as she leaned her back against the fig tree, "you never complain when I lean up against you for hours at a time. You always support me!"

She had always enjoyed the fresh air. As her breathing and heart rate slowed, she let out a long, deep sigh. The sound of chirping birds helped her to relax. The gentle breeze whispered across her face.

When she finally opened her eyes again, she realized that the sun was sinking in the western sky. "Oh, look at you!" she said to the sun. "You've moved!"

She had dozed off again. It seemed to be happening more often in the past few days. *Whenever I close my eyes for more than a minute I fall asleep, and I don't even realize it is happening.*

As she lifted her eyes up to the rocky hills, she thought of one of her favourite scriptures that her Mama, Mary, had taught her from the Torah. She spoke the words aloud to herself, so softly that they were barely audible:

"I will lift up my eyes to the hills

From whence comes my help?

My help comes from the LORD,

Who made heaven and earth."[3]

How she longed to run and dance among the trees and sing the promises of the Torah at the top of her lungs! She remembered dancing with her arms outstretched, and twirling in circles with her eyes lifted toward heaven, feeling the breeze blow her long dark hair. *It would be so splendid to feel healthy and free like I did before… Anyway, it doesn't matter now. The doctor said I'm going to die soon.*

"No!" she shouted at her thoughts. "I will not give up on my life! I will not think about—" She knew that if such thoughts went any further, she would give up what little hope she had left. *Why not think instead about how it was when I was young and healthy and beautiful?*

Thoughts of those blessed days crept into her mind once again. Thirteen years ago, she had been a healthy twelve-year-old, filled with joy and laughter. Her olive skin and slender face marked her as a Jew, even from a distance. As she helped Mama baking bread in the kitchen, or scrubbing laundry in the yard, her face had always glowed with health and happiness.

Life was not easy for them, but although it meant hard work — labouring from dawn to dusk every day, except for the Sabbath — for the most part they did their chores joyfully. Erstis enjoyed going to market, but she looked forward to laundry day the most. On laundry day, she would trudge with Mama and Hannah to the well in the eastern field, and her younger brothers would play in the field behind the well while the women did the washing.

The three women would stand in the blazing heat of the sun and scrub all of the clothes by hand. Erstis' arms and hands would tire from the vigorous scrubbing. The combination of the sun's rays shining down on them and the exertion of energy caused sweat to run down her face and back. After they had laid the clothes on the rocks to dry, they could relax. Erstis would breathe in the fresh scent of grass and wildflowers. That is when they would enjoy the children's laughter as it floated through the air. The birds chirped in the trees, and butterflies fluttered among the flowers.

Many times they would lie on their backs and gaze up at the clouds. They would giggle as they pointed out the different shapes of clouds to each other — a camel here, a sheep over there, a crown, a face, and on and on.

Most mothers wouldn't allow their daughters to talk while they worked. It was believed by many Jewish people that a sombre person was a holy person. Erstis would often remark, "I feel sorry for them, Mama. Talking is what makes the work enjoyable. It's how we share our love with one another."

Erstis would often tell Mama and Hannah of a dramatic daydream that she had imagined, and Hannah and Erstis would both share their dreams of the future with their Mama — dreams of having many children and a happy family.

Mama would tell them what it was like when she fell in love with Papa, and how the evil Henrich tried to get Grandpapa to give Mama in marriage him. That was also when Mama would tell them about the things in the Torah. She would always remind them, "The Torah promises that the Messiah will come one day very soon! He will be King of the Jews and free our people from oppression."

Very few women in their culture knew how to read, because little girls weren't permitted to go to school. Boys sometimes went to school to learn to read and write, and Papa had learned to read when he was a boy. In turn, he had taught Mama to read, and then she taught their children. More importantly, however, she taught them to memorize the scriptures. The Torah was quoted over and over again in their home, especially in the field on laundry days.

The day after laundry day, the skin on her hands would be dried out and cracked. Erstis gashed her knuckles many times when she was first learning to scrub laundry, but the discomfort never bothered her, as she enjoyed the singing, laughing, and dancing that they'd done while working. Mama would soak her daughters' hands in special oil and say, "This will make your hands look like those of a lady of royalty, instead of a Jewish farm girl."

Erstis always felt a tingle go up her spine whenever Papa would caress her smooth hands and tell her, "your hands look as if they belong to a princess."

She fondly recalled the days when papa would return home after being away in the hills. He would be gone for weeks or months at a time. It always seemed that time dragged on and on during his absence. The sun didn't seem to shine as brightly when Papa was away, and the birds didn't chirp as happily. She would listen for his whistle as he walked up the pathway. Then, as she ran to the door, she would shout, "Papa's home! Papa's home!"

She would fling open the door and run down the path to meet him. "There's my girl!" Papa would bellow. He was a husky man with a thickset chest. When he wrapped his muscular arms around her, she felt as though she could hide from every evil of the world, protected by her Papa's arms. Nothing could harm her as long as she had her Papa to save her. She giggled whenever his bushy whiskers tickled her face as he gave her a kiss on the cheek.

Hand-in-hand, they would walk the rest of the way to the house, where Papa would greet Hannah and their little brothers. He

11

always greeted Mama last, and the children were all eager to watch. Without fail, he would whisk her into his arms and whirl her in a circle, lifting her feet right off the floor. Her merry laughter rippled through the family home, mingling with Papa's baritone chuckles and the children's cheers.

Then the boys would tackle them, shouting, "My turn!" and "Me, Papa. Lift me!" until it was impossible to tell who was saying what. Erstis often wondered what people walking past the house might think about the ruckus they heard. Most Jewish homes were solemn and quiet. They were so concerned with their duties that they didn't take the time to fully express the joy and love they had for one another. Many families didn't even stop to think about whether they loved one another. With most betrothals, couples were expected to "grow into" loving one another. Duty was more important than love.

After the sun had set and the boys were snuggled into bed, Hannah and Erstis would join Papa and Mama on the roof. Erstis would close her eyes and sigh as Papa softly played peaceful music on his flute. A smile crossed her lips as she remembered the feeling of life being back to normal again with Papa safely home, at last.Papa would tell them of his journey up into the mountains with the sheep and goats. He always had an exciting tale to tell. Ferocious beasts would sometimes try to attack his animals, or thieves would attempt to steal some of his flock. Many times Erstis would exclaim, "Papa you are the bravest man in the world!"

Papa often said, "Erstis and Hannah, I don't know how it is possible, but I believe you have both grown even more beautiful while I was away."

Erstis knew that she and Hannah were beautiful. When they walked to the market with Mama, they could sense the envy on the other girls' faces. Even some of the mothers would cast an envious look at Mama as if to say, "Why is that woman so blessed? She has two daughters, and both of them are beautiful!"

When Erstis and Hannah went to the town well, the older boys would watch for them to come. They would race each other to be the first to offer to fill the buckets for the young ladies. Although the other girls were jealous, some of them were still friendly to Erstis and Hannah. They were probably hoping to snag the men that Erstis and Hannah didn't choose to be their husbands.

Everyone in town knew that to win the heart of Erstis or Hannah meant that they would receive their hand in marriage. Most families followed the Jewish tradition that the papa decided whom their daughter would marry, based on the man's family name and heritage. In choosing a suitable husband for his daughter, a papa had to consider whether the young man had money, power, and prestige.

Things were different in Erstis' family, however. Erstis and Hannah knew that their Papa wanted the very best for his daughters, and to him that meant love in addition to a good family name. Most families thought the notion of love was ridiculous, but Erstis' Papa had loved her Mama since before they were married, and he had vowed that he would never force his daughters to marry someone they didn't love or approve of.

A movement up in the rocks caught Erstis' eye, and brought her out of her reverie.

A beautiful dove was swooping down into a crevice, and began to coo a soft melody. It reminded her of the last time she saw Moshe.

Moshe... Once again, her thoughts whirled back through the years. Moshe and his sister had been playmates with Erstis and Hannah ever since they were babes. Their mamas were best friends. Naturally, as Erstis and Moshe grew older, their friendship blossomed into deeper feelings of love.

On a beautiful spring day, just after her thirteenth birthday, Erstis' Papa had agreed to give her to Moshe in marriage. The official date for the betrothal was set for the following spring.

In their culture, the betrothal custom was for two papas to agree that their children should be married, usually when the children were still quite young. When the children reached a certain age, they might be introduced to each other — but some couples only met one another for the first time on their wedding day.

Depending on the papas, the children may or may not have had a say in who they married; but nobody would have disrespected their papa by saying that the man or woman he had chosen for them wasn't good enough.

It was different with Erstis and Moshe. Although Erstis' Papa had many offers of marriage for his eldest daughter, he had not made any agreements while she was still a young child. Erstis' and Moshe's parents could all see the love blossoming between them. Then one day Papa decided to take Erstis with him as he took a load of sheep to Moshe's papa, the butcher. Moshe worked with his papa at the shop, so he could learn his papa's trade.

When Erstis and Moshe greeted one another, Papa saw her cheeks flush with pleasure. On their way home that day Papa asked Erstis, "You really like that boy Moshe, don't you?"

Papa watched his daughter blush again.

"Yes, Papa," she whispered.

"You know that it is my duty to choose a suitable husband for you." He saw her nod and look sideways at him. "What would you think if I were to talk to Moshe's papa, to arrange a marriage for you?"

"Oh, Papa!" she gasped as she flung her arms around him, jumping up and down. "You're the best Papa ever! I love you!"

A smile played at her lips as she sat beneath the tree in her half-conscious state, remembering that wonderful day. She could feel her heart beat faster as she remembered how excited she had been when Papa spoke those words.

Moshe's papa was to present a large dowry of riches and gifts for her Papa at the betrothal. It was called the "Mohar." The reason

15

for this custom was that the bride's family was losing a member of the family, while the groom's family was gaining a new member.

Because life was so hard for their people, the loss of a family member decreased the amount of household labour that could be done in a day. The amount of the dowry was to be equivalent to the value of the chores the bride was responsible for within her household. Most papas gave the majority of the Mohar to the bride. A papa who kept the entire Mohar for himself was thought to be unkind and harsh.

There was also the "Mattan," which were gifts that the groom presented to the bride. Because Moshe's papa was a butcher, Erstis' papa knew that even if hard times were to come in the future, Moshe, Erstis, and their family would not go hungry.

A sigh escaped Erstis' lips as her memories shifted back to the last day she'd seen her prince, Moshe. That sunny afternoon, Moshe and Erstis had hiked up the rocky incline.

"I can outrun you and outclimb you any day!" she had bragged. Moshe chuckled and kept right behind her.

When they reached the summit, they sat together under a tree. Quietly, Moshe reached out and took her hand. As she looked up at him, she saw that he was nodding his head in the direction of a cleft in the rock. She followed his gaze, and there a beautiful dove was softly landing and began to coo sweetly.

Moshe turned to Erstis, taking both her hands in his, and softly began to recite a beautiful scripture from the Torah:

> "O my dove, in the clefts of the rock,
> In the secret places of the cliff,
> Let me see your face,
> Let me hear your voice;
> For your voice is sweet,
> And your face is lovely."

The next day, her dreams of a future with Moshe — filled with love, security, and children — had vanished. She had started to bleed. Mama tried to reassure her that it was all part of becoming a woman, and it meant that someday, after she was married to Moshe, she would be blessed with children.

At the time, Erstis thought that the pain in her stomach was the worst thing in the world. Mama said, "In a few more days you will be feeling better, and the bleeding will stop altogether after about six days. Then we will go to the priest to make an offering, and you will be declared 'clean' again." Days later, as Erstis continued to cry in pain, Mama still tried to soothe her by telling her that the bleeding would stop very soon.

It didn't. After ten days, Mama said to Hannah, "Go and bring the doctor to tend to your sister."

When the doctor arrived, he examined the young girl. "She is haemorrhaging," he explained. "There is a medicine we can try. It may help her, but I can't guarantee it will work."

Papa sold three goats to pay for the medicine. To make it worse, the law declared Erstis "ceremonially unclean." If anyone touched her, they would also be declared unclean. They would have to wash their clothes and bathe in water, and even then would still be unclean until evening. Any bed or chair, or anything else Erstis sat on, was also considered to be unclean; and if anyone touched anything that she had sat on, they, too, would be declared unclean.

If anyone came near to her, Erstis had to cry out, "I'm unclean! Do not come near me." People would quickly come to a halt, turn, and walk away from her. They acted like she had a deadly plague. People with this type of illness were usually outcasts and lived outside the city walls, but Papa had built a small hut for Erstis in the back of one of his fields. Nobody passed near her house any more. Even most of the pedlars stayed away. Everyone in the village knew of the dreadful sickness that had changed the beautiful young virgin into what looked like a shrivelled, old woman. At first she felt judged by the community. What evil deed had she done to deserve such punishment? Now she felt forgotten.

I feel so dirty and worthless. It has been twelve long years, and I'm still bleeding. Will it ever stop? She sucked in a breath of air and bit her lip.

Over the years, many different doctors had looked at her to see if they could help her. They always charged high prices for remedies that weren't guaranteed to help. Papa had worked very hard to become wealthy, but when Erstis got sick he used everything he had to pay the doctors' fees until he became a poor man, barely scraping by.

Finally, the sad reality was announced: Erstis would never marry and bear children unless she could be cured. So she agreed to let Papa use her inheritance to buy her more medication, and now she was left in poverty as well. Even if the doctor had something new to offer her, she would have had no money left to buy it.

In the early days of her illness, each time she tried a new medicine, her family all hoped and prayed the bleeding would stop. If it had stopped, they would have counted seven days, and then on the eighth day, she would take two turtle doves or two young pigeons to the priest as a sin offering and a burnt offering. However, the bleeding never did stop — it only got worse. Erstis had never been able to go to the priest to make her offerings and be declared clean.

Her beautiful, taut, olive skin had now been left ghostly white, due to the loss of so much blood. Her long, satiny black hair was falling out, and what little hair was left was very light in colour. Because she had lost so much weight, her bones protruded from the sagging folds of her skin. If someone were to see her for the first time, they would think she was a wrinkled old lady, rather than the twenty-five-year-old that she was.

She didn't even resemble the same person who had climbed the hill with Moshe twelve years ago. Because she was unclean, the law prohibited her from mingling with people in public. One glance at her, and people would know that she was sick and unclean. "The boys at the water well wouldn't jump to help me now," she said to herself. "They'd run away from me!"

When the changes first started, she was overwhelmed with shame at her appearance. Now, her looks didn't bother her. Although there were no looking glasses in her little hut, she knew that she was ugly, especially compared to her former beauty.

The sickness overcame what little vanity she may have had. Continuous stabs of pain in her abdomen, combined with the waves of nausea and vomiting, threatened to take over her body. Volts of pain tore at the muscles in her back from the violent heaving — but the thing that really frightened her were the frequent dizzy spells, which merged into extreme weakness and loss of consciousness. When the spells first started, they would only last for several minutes — but now, almost every day, she would lose consciousness for hours at a time.

"One of these days," the doctor had warned her, "you will not regain consciousness."

As dusk settled in about her, she groaned and shifted her position on the cushion. "You're not as comfortable as you used to be," she told the cushion. "Then again, it could be that I'm skin and bones everywhere, even on my bottom."

She laboured to get up off her cushion. *I'd better go inside before I freeze.*

Her muscles and joints ached most of the day. She found it especially painful when she tried to stand after sitting or lying in the same position for a long time. She drew in a deep breath, savouring the aroma of the wildflowers, and sound of the birds chirping in the trees. Slowly she turned toward her little hut.

She patted the tree with her hand. "See you tomorrow, Miss Te'enah. Thanks for your help."

How she dreaded being shut inside. She consoled herself with thoughts of the relative comfort she would feel as she lowered herself onto her bedroll after the seemingly long trek to her home.

"Lord, help me," she breathed.

She set her mouth firmly and determinedly as she put one foot in front of the other, taking one slow step at a time. As she trudged along, each step seemed to be more laborious than the one before. *What does it matter?* she wondered. *I won't be alive much longer, anyway.* She shook her head slightly to get rid of the discouraging thought.

She sighed aloud. "Forgive me, Lord. I'm very thankful that I'm not stuck in the catacombs like some of the unclean. Thank you, Yaweh,[5] for my loving family."

Then she heard it — like a peaceful, quiet wind. The Voice of Promise spoke to her. "You have found favour in the eyes of the Lord. Because of your great faith, generation after generation will glorify the Lord G-d of Israel."

When she had first heard His voice, many years ago, she had jerked her head from side-to-side searching for the person who spoke to her. The voice was seemingly audible, yet there was no one near her to speak the words. Over the years, she began to wonder whether, if there had been anyone else with her at the time, would they have heard the voice as well?

21

She knew the voice was real. She didn't imagine it. She really did hear it. Although she didn't quite know who the voice belonged to, she had secretly named it the "Voice of Promise." She no longer looked around when she heard the voice.

Yet, I don't understand how this can be the favour of the Lord? And what great faith do I have, anyway?

As a child, she had no idea what the Voice of Promise was talking about. Then, when she heard the voice during the first few months of her sickness, she realized that it had given her great faith that Jehovah Rapha would heal her.[6] She would send messages to Moshe, "Do not worry, my dear. I will soon be well, and then we will be wed. We will have many children to fill our home with love and laughter."

As time wore on, she stopped sending messages. When her sister or Mama told her that Moshe had asked about her, she would reply, "Tell him to forget about me. He should get on with his life and marry another. I will never be well!" It was clear that she was not living a life of favour in anyone's eyes, let alone those of the G-d of Israel.

Eventually, she settled into the quiet and lonely life of an outcast. The anger passed and her faith was renewed. "There must be a reason the Voice of Promise keeps whispering to me," she would remind herself. "The Lord must have a special purpose for my life, even if I cannot comprehend what it could be, or how it would affect generation after generation. Perhaps the Messiah will come in my generation and will deliver me from my sickness."

22

When she finally reached her living space, she weakly mixed herself another fortified drink and sipped it slowly. With a sigh of exhaustion, she lay down on her bedroll. As she closed her eyes, the scaly demon of Fear placed his black claws on her chest. He slowly pushed down, and then he increased the pressure on her chest. Fear gripped her heart. He whispered, "Will you wake up tomorrow?"

She gasped. Her heart beat faster. Her skin felt cool. She shivered. It hurt to inhale. Her thoughts began to race. Was this really her last day to live? Who would find her dead body? What would happen to her after she died? An evil grin spread across Fear's face.

Suddenly, a flash of light appeared in the room. Fear jerked his head to the left, and released his hold on Erstis. In the corner was Hope — a tall, bright, angelic being holding out a gleaming sword pointed directly at him.

"Be gone!" Hope demanded in a booming voice.

In an instant, Fear flew out of the hut and across the sky toward a distant dark hill. Hope sheathed his sword and walked over to Erstis' cool, clammy body. He gently rested his hand on her chest.

Erstis took a deep breath. A smile formed on her lips as she realized that — no matter what might happen tomorrow — G-d would be with her. She mentally recited the prayer that Mama had taught her many years ago:

Tammy Leigh Robinson

Have mercy on me,
O JEHOVAH, for I am in trouble;
My eye wastes away with grief,
Yes, my soul and my body!
For my life is spent with grief,
And my years with sighing;
My strength fails because of my iniquity,
And my bones waste away.
I am a reproach among all my enemies,
But especially among my neighbours,
And am repulsive to my acquaintances;
Those who see me outside flee from me.
I am forgotten like a dead man, out of mind;
I am like a broken vessel.
For I hear the slander of many;
Fear is on every side;
But as for me, I trust in You, O JEHOVAH;
I say, "You are my Eloheem."
Be of good courage,
And He shall strengthen your heart,
All you who hope in JEHOVAH."[7]

CHAPTER TWO

The Clean Leper

(Mark 1:40-45)

Late the next morning, Erstis opened her eyes when she heard footsteps crunching down the path toward her small hut. Her heart leapt within her. *I'm alive!* She smiled as she realized it. *And someone is coming to visit!*

But just as suddenly as her heart had leapt, it then plummeted. She wondered if her visitor was a passing pedlar who didn't know that she was unclean. Even though her hut was set in the back field on her Papa's property, a few travelling pedlars would still dare to come to her door, desperate for a sale. When people drew near her, she would have to shout, "I'm unclean! Do not come near!" Jewish customs dictated that when the door of a home was closed, it meant there was trouble and visitors were not welcome. If everything was well, the door would be open. However, some pedlars were so desperate to sell their wares that they disregarded the unspoken rules of etiquette. Erstis supposed it wasn't their fault.

Other people in her situation would be shunned by their families, as well as being shunned by society. Unclean people were usually forced to live outside the city. Still, she dreaded facing the teenage boys who loved to walk by her hut and taunt her.

Erstis' family was an exception to the rules of Jewish society. Her father had contributed substantially to the restoration of the city gate, among other improvements to the city and the temple. Because of his social influence, he had been permitted to build the small hut for her, in the back of one of his fields.

When Erstis first moved into the small hut, she felt as though the hours dragged by. She had grown up in a large family, so she was used to having people around her all the time. Now her humble home was dead quiet, except for twice a week when someone in the family would come to bring water or milk. She could only imagine what it must be like for the people who lived outside the city. Most of them never saw their families ever again. *Poor souls. At least I have a family to be thankful for.*

Coming back from her drifting thoughts, she whispered to herself, "Maybe I should leave my door closed, and not answer their call. But what if it is someone in the family? If only I could remember what day it is. It must be milk day. It is probably Cousin Ruth bringing me milk. Bless her, Yahweh, for her faithfulness!"

Cousin Ruth was born only ten days before Erstis. The two girls had grown up treating each other like sisters. When they were children, it seemed as though Ruth spent more time at Erstis' home than she did at her own. Their childhood had been filled with joy, health, and innocence.

Just then, she heard Ruth call out a cheerful greeting. Erstis slowly approached the doorway and raised her heavy hand, slightly, to wave to her guest. She leaned against the doorpost to wait for Ruth to come closer.

They exchanged customary blessings but, as usual, omitted the traditional kiss. Then Ruth carried the bucket of milk into the shack. Being cautious not to touch anything, she poured the milk into the clay jar that was kept in the corner.

Meanwhile, Ertstis worked hard to keep her emotions under control. It had been twelve long years since she had received a hug — she had not even felt the lightest pressure of a hand resting on her arm for reassurance. It seemed like such a long time. *Oh, how I wish I had someone to hold me*, she lamented silently.

She missed being out in public, too. She had enjoyed going to the Synagogue and the market. As she had wandered around, voices and laughter mingled together. There was very little joy and laughter in her life now.

She released a long, deep sigh as she prayed. *Thank you, Lord, for my family. Without them I would be utterly alone and living in the catacombs outside the city.*

"Would you like to sit out back for a few minutes?" Ruth asked. She placed her hand protectively over her blossoming womb.

29

Erstis, being sure to keep her distance, squeezed her hands into tight fists at her sides. It was like they had a mind of their own. Even after all these years of not being able to touch anyone, her hands still longed to reach out. She gave them an especially hard squeeze, as if to tell them to stay in their proper place.

She sighed deeply, looking into her cousin's eyes. It was clear by the firm set of Erstis' jaw that she was torn. She loved her cousin dearly, but was concerned about the health of her unborn child. It had taken years for Ruth and Joseph to get pregnant, and then they had lost their first baby before it even had time to grow strong enough to be delivered from the womb.

Now that she was pregnant again, Erstis, the doctor, and the family had all advised Ruth not to visit her unclean cousin. They hoped to prevent possible infection to the unborn child. Ruth, however, refused to believe that her miscarriage was related to Erstis' illness. As much as she loved her unborn child, she also loved Erstis, and she continued to visit her all the same.

"Sure," Erstis responded, "I could rest for a little while." She weakly leaned on the front door while she waited for Ruth to exit.

Because Erstis was unclean, it was especially important for Ruth not to touch her, nor anything that she might have touched.

As they made their way to the back yard, Erstis wistfully remembered the times when she had walked hand-in-hand with Ruth. She hadn't realized what a blessing it was to reach out and hold a hand of a loved one while walking beside them. She still remembered the warmth and softness of holding hands. Unless she recovered, she would never experience that feeling ever again.

Erstis recalled being able to sit down inside her Mama's home to have a refreshing drink with their company. Now, she had to take her visitors outside behind the hut. Along with her own cushioned seat, Papa had placed a second seat for her guests to rest on. It was a "clean" chair, which meant Erstis had not touched it — and would not.

She thought back to when she was a child. The Jewish custom of greeting was to embrace one another in a warm hug, and give each other a light kiss — known as the holy kiss — on each cheek. She sighed as she realized how long it had been since someone had hugged or kissed her.

She remembered when Papa would wrap his burly arms around her. It had made her feel safe and secure. A shiver ran through her body at the memory. Her eyes burned. They would have filled with tears, had she been healthy enough for her glands to produce tears. She ached for human touch. At times, her longing seemed harder to bear than her physical pain and weakness.

Several minutes later, when Ruth and Erstis were settled out back, Ruth asked what the doctor had said at his last visit. Erstis sighed softly as the words haunted her again. "It won't be much longer now," she said in barely a whisper.

"He must be wrong!" Ruth cried. She leaned closer to Erstis and gestured toward her. "Look at you! You haven't changed a bit in the last year. You just need to keep drinking your milk and herbal mixture and you'll be better soon. You'll see! Maybe there is another doctor that can look at you." She placed her hand on her bulging belly. "Besides, the baby will be born in two months and he'll want his Auntie Erstis to play with him and watch him grow up."

"Ruth," Erstis sympathized, "I know this is hard for you. Yet, you need to face the truth. I am getting weaker every day. I lose consciousness for minutes and even hours at a time. Soon I won't wake up from my sleep. Please focus on your baby, Ruth. You need to be strong for him and Joseph. You know I love you and I want what is best for you. You need to accept this."

Tears filled Ruth's eyes. She looked away as she bit her trembling lip. Tears spilled down her cheeks as she sobbed. "But you haven't shed a tear! You're very strong, even if your body belies the fact."

Erstis shook her head slightly and lowered her eyes to the ground. The fountain of emotion that welled up within her was now threatening to spill over. She wished Ruth understood that the lack of tears did not constitute strength, or the lack of despair. Yes, she trusted Yahweh to do what was best, but her body was drying up. She was physically unable to cry.

Erstis lifted her head. "I haven't enough fluid in my body to shed a single tear," she explained. With a deep breath she

32

smiled and continued, "But that's enough about me. How is Joseph doing?"

Ruth dabbed at her tears with a delicately stitched handkerchief as she took several deep breaths to calm her sobs. "He's doing well," she replied. "He has finished making the baby's bed."

Erstis' smile grew wider. "That's wonderful! Tell me, is there any news from town?"

They lived in Magadan, a small town near the north shore of the Sea of Galilee. It consisted of farming families where goats and sheep wandered about the pasture. Many farms also had fields of wheat, barley, and other grains.

Magadan was south of Capernaum, a much larger village. During special feasts, they would go to the Synagogue in Capernaum to worship. Erstis knew she would not have the strength to make the long trek to Capernaum now. It took the whole morning to walk there. They would have to sleep there until the end of the feast. The next morning they would set out at dawn to return home.

For the weekly Sabbaths, the family worshipped at the local Synagogue in Magadan. Thoughts of the Sabbath and the Synagogue brought sadness to Erstis. As a young girl, she had loved going to the Synagogue to worship with others, and she enjoyed listening to the reading of the Torah. For the past twelve years, she hadn't been allowed to go, because she was unclean. She had hoped the bleeding would stop so she could take her offering to the priest and make atonement for her flow of blood. She sighed as she realized that she would probably never set foot in the Synagogue again.

She remembered hurrying to get ready for the Sabbath. It would start a few minutes before the sun set. The family gathered around the dinner table. Mama would cover her head with the prayer shawl and light the candles, and then she would say the prayers of Shabbat. After that, Papa would say his prayers in his thundering voice. Finally, they would all sing, "Shabbat Shalom! Shabbat Shalom! Shabbat, Shabbat, Shabbat, Shabbat Shaolm!"[8] They would clap their hands and dance around as they sang about the Sabbath Peace.

Shabbat was a time to celebrate the creation of the world. When the Lord created the earth, He did it all in six days, and then He rested on the seventh day. Therefore, Shabbat was a day to be free from work. It was time to rest and meditate on the wonders of Yahweh.

"Oh, yes!" Ruth's voice brought Erstis out of her reverie. Ruth's face suddenly brightened, and Erstis turned her attention back to Ruth. "The most amazing thing happened! You know the leper, here in Magadan? Remember that he contracted the disease just the year before you got sick?"

When she saw Erstis nod slightly, Ruth continued, "Well you're never going to believe this, but he was healed!"

"Healed?" Erstis asked, as her brows furrowed with her slight frown. "What do you mean *healed*? There is no cure for leprosy." Erstis gasped. *How could he be made whole?*

Unseen by Ruth and Erstis sitting in the field, a flash of light rushed across the sky. The angel of Hope arrived and started to fill Erstis' heart with thoughts of how her life would change if she were healed. Seconds later, however, the demon of Doubt flew in behind him. Doubt silently slashed his dark sword toward Hope.

Hope sensed the evil presence behind him, and quickly spun around. Before Doubt's black sword could strike him, he brought his bright sword against it in a resounding clang.

Erstis and Ruth were oblivious to the struggle of the two spiritual beings. The angel and the demon moved about the field, their swords clashing. Each being was intent on being rid of the other, so he could have clear access to Erstis. They flew up into the sky, then dove down to the earth, and darted around the field, slashing at each other.

"You see," Ruth continued, "a stranger named Yeshua[9] has arrived from Nazareth. People say He has been healing people and casting out devils. The leper heard about Him. Then someone told him that Yeshua was going to be near the Sea of Galilee. Can you believe he walked all that way to find Him? It must have taken him at least a whole day!" Ruth waved her hands in the air, as if she couldn't believe it herself.

"That is against the law!" gasped Erstis as she sat up in her seat. "Lepers must camp *outside* the city. They aren't permitted to mix with other people in public places. Didn't the people around him see that he was a leper? He broke the Law of Moses. He could have been stoned!" Unnoticed by the two women, the battle between Hope and Doubt raged on.

"I suppose he was willing to take that risk," Ruth said with a shrug of her shoulders. "He really believed that if he could just get to Him, this Yeshua could make him well. But that's not the most amazing part." She leaned forward, forgetting that she must not get too close to Erstis. "Listen to this!"

"I'm trying to, if you would just tell the story." Erstis also leaned forward, ignoring the pain knotting in her stomach. She felt a stirring deep inside her soul. Hope gouged his dagger into the outer layer of Doubt's tough, scaly skin. A steady stream of putrid green ooze flowed out of the wound.

"When the leper saw Yeshua, he knelt down, and implored Him, 'If you are willing, You can make me clean.' Do you know what the Nazarene did?" queried Ruth.

"Did He turn away from him? Or did He condemn him?" Erstis guessed. Doubt lunged at Hope.

"No! They say He looked at the leper with compassion, like you've never seen before. Then..." she said as she unknowingly reached out her hand toward Erstis, "He reached out... and *touched* him!"

36

"What?" Erstis cried as she pulled back from Ruth. "He... touched... him?" She hardly dared to believe it. In a flash of light Hope quickly jumped aside, taking an enormous slice out of the demon as he did so. Doubt roared as a black cloud spewed forth from him.

"Yes! Can you believe it? He *touched* the leper!" asserted Ruth. She sat on the edge of her seat. "Then He said, 'I am willing; be cleansed.' As soon as He said that... the leprosy left!" she shouted, as she jumped up off her chair. She was so excited by the story that she momentarily forgot about the extra weight she carried around her midsection.

She started walking around, waving her hands in the air as she did so. "Every bit of it was gone! Right in front of hundreds of people! The strange thing is that this man Yeshua warned him not to say anything to anyone. He told him to go on his way, show himself to the priest, and offer what Moses commanded. I'm sure that as soon as he went to the priest, he went about telling everyone what happened to—"

"How do you know this?" demanded Erstis, interrupting her cousin. She sat back in her chair.

"Joseph told me. He was there! He saw it with his own eyes. He told me every word. What do you think of that?" asked Ruth with a fling of her hand, as if she had just placed some physical evidence in front of Erstis.

"I... I... don't know... what... to think." Erstis stammered. "It... it's unheard of!"

37

Hope pushed Doubt against a tree. His strong arms pinned him there. Hope glared into Doubt's eerie yellow eyes. It was time to let this oozing creature know who was boss. He took a step back as he swiftly brought the point of his sword up to Doubt's throat. The tip of his sword was starting to pierce his rubbery skin. In that split-second Doubt put the flat of his right foot on the tree behind him. Using the tree as leverage, he pushed himself right into Hope. The momentum of his body knocked Hope to the ground. Hope landed on his back.

Doubt dove on top of Hope. His claw-like hand wrapped around Hope's throat, and began to squeeze it. Hope managed to raise his sword just enough to slice into Doubt's back. Doubt cried out in agony and unknowingly loosened his hand. That was the chance Hope needed to push Doubt off of him. They both scrambled to their feet.

"What do you think, Ruth?" asked Erstis. She knew that Ruth's husband, Joseph, was a devout Jew. He was a trustworthy man, but the story seemed too preposterous to believe — no matter who had seen it!

Ruth threw her hands up in the air. "I'm amazed! I think He must be the Messiah!"

Erstis gasped. She raised her hand to cover her mouth. Ruth walked straight toward her, as if she would reach out and take hold of both her hands.

"Who else would have the power to heal deadly diseases, and cast out devils? If He's not the Messiah, then He must be crazy. Only a crazy man would touch a leper! Joseph said he will go to find out whatever he can about this Nazarene stranger."

Erstis leaned forward again and fired off questions in rapid succession. "Why haven't we heard about Him before? Who is He? Is He an old man? Maybe He *is* crazy. Is He married?"

In the same moment, Doubt quickly slashed his sword back and forth toward Hope. Suddenly, he sliced into Hope's upper arm. Swiftly Hope dashed away from Doubt.

Ruth whispered in a conspiratorial tone, "Well, the only thing I know about Him is the talk that is going around the village. I haven't actually seen Him yet, but I heard that His father is Joseph the Carpenter."

"Do you mean the man Papa bought that handsome table from? The one for Mama's dowry?" asked Erstis, in a somewhat hushed tone.

"The very same!" Ruth declared.

"Well, He can't be very old, then." Erstis' head was bent in thought for a moment, before she returned her gaze to Ruth. "What does his wife think about Him touching lepers?"

"No, he's not old. He's only in his early thirties. And His wife doesn't care what He does, because He's not married!"

"What?" Erstis' eyebrows shot up. "He's thirty, and he's not married? What's wrong with him? He must be crazy!"

39

Ruth frowned. "That's what I wondered, too. But Joseph said he looked normal enough. He said He takes a long time to think before He speaks. Joseph also said that when He looks at you..." Ruth wistfully clutched her hands together at her breast. She closed her eyes and let out a deep sigh. "... it seems like He's looking right into your soul. It's like He sees every bad thing you've ever done, but..." her voice trailed off.

A moment later, she opened her eyes and let her hands drop to her side. "The strange thing is that He doesn't seem to condemn you. Joseph said that He looks at you with love and compassion." Ruth walked back to her seat and sat down, as if she was so astounded by what she had just said that she couldn't stand up any longer.

Erstis leaned back to rest on her cushion. "He sounds eccentric to me," she commented.   Now Doubt leapt out from behind a tree, catching Hope off guard. His sword tore a jagged gash into Hope's stomach. Hope darted away.

"Perhaps He is. I heard He is very wise. The Scribes and Pharisees try to trick Him by asking Him loaded questions. But He always outsmarts them. Joseph said it's almost like He *knows* what they're thinking." said Ruth, thoughtfully. She furrowed her brow as she tried to comprehend the reality of her own words.

"But... how could that be? Unless... He *is* the Messiah!" gasped Erstis, jerking to attention at the possibility. A shiver ran through her body. *Could the Messiah actually have come to deliver Israel during my lifetime?*

40

Doubt tried to jab Hope with the pommel of his sword, but Hope flew out of the way, causing Doubt to lose his balance. In a flash, with all his strength, Hope swung his sword downwards towards Doubt, who was sprawled across the ground. He sliced off one of Doubt's limbs, and a putrid green discharge gushed out from the wound.

With a shake of her head, Ruth said, "I'm not sure what to think. I heard He stays on the outskirts of the village now. He wanders around on lonely roads. Yet hundreds, even thousands of people still go out to see Him. They come from all over. Some travel for days just to reach Him. Some want to be healed, some like to listen to Him speak, and some just want to find out *who* He is. I think I'll ask Mama if she wants to go with me to see Him tomorrow..." She babbled on, not realizing that her words were tearing her dear cousin's heart to shreds.

Erstis' heart longed to be free from her invisible prison, so she could also go to see the man that performed miracles. She was prisoner in her own home, since it was against the law for her to go out in public. Even more heartbreaking was the prison within the prison — not being able to touch another human being. She smiled and said to Ruth, "Please tell me everything you find out about Him."

"Oh, of course I will." She stood to her feet and, preparing to leave, straightened her skirts. "Actually, Mama will come to bring you water in two days' time. She will tell you all about it when she comes."

"Must you leave?" asked Erstis. She couldn't describe the feelings that were stirring inside her, but she knew it had to something to do with the news of the young man called Yeshua. She wanted to ask Ruth more about Him.

"Yes, dear Erstis. I need to be going now. Be sure to get some rest. May Yahweh be with you and bless you." Ruth waved as she turned to walk toward the road.

Erstis watched her cousin walk away. Her mind was racing.

Doubt and Hope continued to wage war over her soul. The putrid green stream continued to spew out from where Doubt had lost his limb. Hope lunged again at Doubt, but Doubt leapt aside. Hope went tumbling to the ground. Doubt dove through the air towards the sprawled form.

Erstis' mind was racing as she reviewed what her cousin had said. *He was willing to touch the unclean leper.* She wondered whether the story must have been made up — it may have just been gossip. *Surely, there couldn't be any truth to it. Who would touch a leper?*

Hope adeptly blocked Doubt's attack. Catching Doubt for a moment, he sent him sailing backwards through the air. The black, winged figure had the wind knocked out of him as he hit the ground.

Erstis thought of Joseph. *He wouldn't lie. He isn't like that. He's a devout Jew.* She laid her head back and closed her eyes, as Peace swooped in and flooded her soul. *He didn't condemn the leper for breaking the law, but looked at him with compassion. When was the last time someone looked at me with compassion instead of pity?* She remembered that it had been on her final day spent with Moshe, long ago.

Unwilling to dwell on that blessed memory, for fear of sadness stealing upon her, she sighed and heaved her weak body to a standing position. As usual, the world went whirling around her. She leaned against Miss Te'enah for a moment, until her vision came back into focus. Then, with great determination, she slowly put one foot in front of the other, until finally she made it back to her little dwelling.

Upon entering her home, she leaned against the wall to take a few deep breaths, and to regain some strength to continue. She knew that she was getting weaker every day, but she told herself she just needed to drink some of the milk and herbal mixture, and then she would feel a little bit better.

The thought pushed her to grab her mug and fill it with creamy white milk from the clay jar. She mixed in a scoop of the dry mix, and took the mug with her to her bedroll, where she flopped down to take her nourishing but distasteful drink.

Meanwhile, Doubt was regaining consciousness. When he opened his eyes, Hope was standing over him with the point of his dagger piercing his black throat. With a booming voice, Hope ordered him, "Leave this place, before I tear you to shreds!"

Instantly, Hope pulled the dagger back. Doubt slithered away from Hope, flapped his black wings, and flew far away into the distance leaving an acrid odour in his wake. Swiftly, Hope rushed back to his charge. He found Erstis half lying, half sitting on her bed, sipping from her mug, mindless of the white drops of milk that spilled onto her clothes. Lightly he flew over to join his fellow angel, Peace. They ministered to her spirit, filling her thoughts with words of hope and peace.

A bud of hope started blossoming within her. *How could this be? The leprosy left that man immediately! Yeshua must be the Messiah!* Slowly, placing the mug on the hard-packed dirt floor, she lay down and closed her eyes with a wistful sigh.

As sleep overcame her frail body, she saw two beautiful eyes, filled with compassion like she had never seen before. She felt as if those eyes were boring into the depths of her soul, reading the pain, the doubt, the questions, the faith, and the hope that dwelt therein. Yet, in those eyes that drew her to Him, there was not even the slightest hint of condemnation — only compassion.

CHAPTER THREE

The Walking Paralytic

Mark 2:1-12

Two days later, before the sun stretched its fingers across the land, Erstis was lying on her bedroll. She had been awake for some time — her stiff, aching body not moving, and her dry eyes staring straight up at the flat, clay roof. Her breathing was so shallow that her chest appeared not to rise and fall. The only sign of life was the occasional blink of her eyes, but her body was withering away to the point where there wasn't enough fluid to moisten her eyes. With each blink, her eyelids would scratch roughly across the surface of her eyes, causing irritation and redness.

Invisible to the human eye, Hope and Peace had been standing in a dark corner all night, praying for their delicate charge. They watched as the leathery black figure of Depression massaged her temples, filling her mind with thoughts of defeat and death. "You aren't going to get any better," he whispered. "The doctor told you it's just a matter of time before you'll be dead. You're barely alive now. Why not just give up? Why keep fighting, when you're just going to die anyway? Just close your eyes. You're almost gone now. Just relax. Let go of the fight... Let it happen naturally..."

In his eagerness to help Erstis, Hope took a step forward, but Peace thrust out a strong arm across his chest. His eyes told Hope to be patient. Erstis had to face this attack alone. They could not intervene until she called out to Yahweh for help.

As Depression became sure that he had won the battle, his sharp talons increased their pressure, digging deeply into her temples. He began to call out for Death to come to her. Before his call could escape his lips, however, a barely audible sound came from the lifeless form lying on the bedroll. "Father... Yahweh..." was the only thing that Erstis had the strength to cry.

In a brilliant flash of light, Hope came out from the dark corner, and sent Depression sprawling on the hard packed earth. With a thud, he landed in a black heap. Simultaneously, Peace leapt to the side of the pitiful form, and soothed her spirit.

Scrambling around, Depression got up on his feet, drawing his sword. The large demon was not as quick as the smaller ones. His specialty was preparing the victim for the call of Death. He would go to work when the angels weren't expecting him, and he did his best work during the night. Often he could accomplish his dirty deed before the first ray of dawn split across the eastern sky.

Now, however, there was an electric charge in the air. It had started when the Son of Yahweh came to earth. Lucifer, the Father of Lies, had called a meeting to decide what to do about Yeshua. The small black Schemer, together with his wimpy sidekick Betrayer, had devised an outstanding plot to put an end to Him.

48

It appeared to the dark assembly that Yeshua was healing the sick and casting out demons, thereby bringing more and more glory to Yahweh. The only way to prevent Him from gaining more approval and fame among mankind was to kill the sick people before the time came for them to meet Yeshua. That is how Depression came to be in Erstis' hut. He was working his craft with the plan of killing her before she got the crazy notion that she should go see the Messiah for herself.

Depression's eyes were wild. He looked from side to side, assessing the number of heavenly beings. He didn't see his companions — Doubt and Death — just yet. His black eyes took in the status of the job ahead; but unknown to him, a host of heavenly warriors were posted around the little cabin, to keep out all other evil-workers.

Depression could only see Hope and Peace. He thought he could handle the two angels on his own. Besides, by the time he was done with them, Doubt and Death would arrive to finish the job on Erstis. With that assurance in mind, he put up his sword to block a blow from Hope. The power behind the blow was more forceful than he had prepared for. It sent him flying through the air again.

The two engaged in a quick battle, one favoured by wit, the other favoured by the power of prayer. Meanwhile, Peace soothed Erstis' mind. He reminded her of the promises in the Torah. The peace of Yahweh began to flood her soul.

Swiftly, two more angelic beings, Strength and Desire, swooped into the room. They headed straight for the small lump

49

in the bedroll, where they joined Peace. Strength was needed to overcome the damage Depression had done. Desire was there to give her the initiative to step outside her comfort zone and imagine the impossible becoming possible. As they ministered the Word of Yahweh to her, she began to pray silently.

Suddenly, like a spark busting into a great flame, the room was filled with light. Erstis couldn't see that the glory of Yahweh filled the room in answer to her prayers. With a resounding clang, Depression dropped his sword and quickly brought his arms up to shield his eyes from the blinding light. From the pit of his evil belly, he let out a blood-curdling scream that rippled across the spiritual realm. The bright light filled his vision with white spots. He stumbled about, looking for his fallen sword. It was hopeless. The white light was blinding him. He squeezed his eyes shut.

In haste, he flew out through the flat-roofed house, leaving a fetid trail of black smoke streaming behind him. As he broke free of the small dwelling, he spotted the host of angels. At breakneck speed, he bolted for Lucifer's secret den. The demons had been hiding there ever since they had first heard of Yeshua's presence.

Moving quickly, Hope joined the other three that were gathered about Erstis, and together the four glorified beings began to comfort her. Each one gave her some of his power. This child was very important to the Master. The Father would receive great glory as a result of her faith. The enemy must not be allowed to spoil His plans.

Erstis felt excitement welling up within her as Peace whispered into her ear, "It has been two days since cousin Ruth's visit. Today is the day that Aunt Rachel will bring water! She will bring news of the extraordinary man called Yeshua."

Erstis let her mind wander back to the events of the day before. Yesterday, she had been lounging in her chair in a shady spot behind her little hut. Suddenly, in the heat of the day, she heard shouts and cries. "He's coming! Yeshua is coming! He's down by the water! Hurry! Hurry! Let's go!" She had seen hundreds of people running down the road toward the water's edge.

She wasn't aware of it, but Desire had pushed her to a standing position. Strength caused the blood to surge through her veins, like it hadn't in years. Hope and Desire carried her swiftly forward. Within seconds, she found herself in her front yard. It was as if her feet hadn't even touched the ground. Her body, which normally felt heavy and weak, had felt like it was floating on air.

Hope had whispered encouragement into her ear, "He's come to town! He healed the leper. He can heal you too! You must go see Him!" The thoughts rushed through Erstis' mind as she hurried onward. Without realizing it, she had reached out her thin, unclean hand to the front gate that signified her imprisoned life of sickness and uncleanness. If she had touched the gate, it would have to be declared unclean, and then would be destroyed by fire.

51

Suddenly, Doubt and Fear had swooped down from out of nowhere, knocking Hope and Desire to the ground in twin heaps. As Desire fell, the tip of Fear's sword gashed his left arm. Erstis stopped short, as if she had hit a brick wall. She had been only a handbreadth away from touching the gate when Doubt had flown back to hiss into her ear, "You're unclean! You can't go to Him! They'll stone you to death!"

Erstis gasped and brought her hand up to her heart. She envisioned the townspeople dragging her to the centre of town, throwing heavy stones at her frail body. Fear had shouted into her ear, "Turn around! Run inside! Don't let them see you. You need to hide!" Turning with unusual agility, she had hurried back into her small house.

Just then, Hope and Desire recovered from their sudden blows. As Desire was struggling to get up, Fear came in a black blur and took a swipe at Hope with his sword — but Hope had seen him coming. He parried the attack, then quickly jumped up again and took a flying leap at Doubt. Desire flew aside to tend to his wound while the other white and black figures engaged in a battle of clanging swords.

Though unaware of the supernatural struggle that had raged around her, Erstis was in a state of shock at what had just transpired at the gate. She flopped onto her bedroll as dry sobs shook her small frame. After only a few minutes, sleep had overcome her.

Now, as she lay on her bedroll reflecting on the happenings of the day before, she began to feel that same pulsing in her veins. The blood felt like it was flowing properly. She hadn't felt that strong since... well, she couldn't remember when! She wondered why she felt so strong. *Was I actually running? Yes, I was! But I haven't been able to run in ten years...*

As Strength laid his hands upon her lungs, Erstis breathed a deep breath of life. She sat up. A smile spread across her lips. She sensed expectancy in the air. Maybe it was just because Yeshua was in town. Or perhaps it was because Aunt Rachel was going to come over today. She didn't know why, but she went cheerfully about her little hut, humming a Psalm to herself.

Before long, she heard the familiar call from Aunt Rachel. "Hello! Erstis, it's Aunt Rachel. I'm here!"

Erstis went out to the yard to greet her Aunt. They exchanged blessings, avoiding the traditional holy kiss, as usual.

"Erstis, you're looking well today," said Aunt Rachel.

"Thank you," she replied. "I am feeling quite well right now. Earlier, before I got up, I felt absolutely dreadful. I thought I should die, lying there on my bedroll."

"Oh!" gasped Aunt Rachel, "Don't speak of such things, my dear. You don't want to tempt fate! Besides, how could one go from feeling that badly, to looking as radiant as you do now?"

"Radiant?" queried Erstis, as she led Aunt Rachel to the water bucket. Aunt Rachel poured the water into Erstis' bucket, being careful not to touch anything in the hut.

"Why yes! There's almost a glow about you. If I didn't know better, I'd think you were a new bride, or an expectant mother! You're positively glowing!"

Erstis could feel her cheeks growing warm under the praises of her charming Aunt. They looked like two bright red apples against her stark white skin. Lost in thought, she realized, *I haven't blushed since the enchanting day when Moshe...*

Peace extended his brawny arm to Strength. The Father had granted that they could give Erstis a small bit of added strength, because of her cry out to Him. Peace shot a look at Strength as if to say, "Take it easy. Don't overdo it. You're not the Master, you know."

Erstis led Aunt Rachel to the backyard, where they could recline for a while. After Erstis was settled in her seat, and Aunt Rachel was settled on the guest cushion, Erstis put forth the question that had been burning inside of her. "So, tell me, have you and Cousin Ruth been to see Yeshua the Nazarene?"

At Aunt Rachel's slight nod, Erstis edged forward on her seat, and queried excitedly, "Well, what do you think of Him? Please tell me everything!"

"It was the most amazing thing I have ever seen," began Aunt Rachel. "As we walked to the house near the water's edge, where He was, we noticed that hundreds of people were coming from every direction. What an incredible sight! It was almost like being in Jerusalem during the Feast of the Passover."

"Yes, I know," cut in Erstis. "I couldn't help being drawn by the crowd passing by yesterday. It sounded like there were people coming from every town of Galilee, Judea, and Jerusalem. Surely they couldn't all fit into one house?"

"Oh my, no!" exclaimed Aunt Rachel. "They spilled out into the streets, as far as the eye could see! Ruth and I had set out early, so we were among the blessed ones. We were right inside the doorway."

"Ohhh!" breathed Erstis. "So you could see Him up close? What was He like? Was He kind and gentle, or was He strong and full of authority?"

"Well..." mused Aunt Rachel, "I'd have to say that He was both. To look at Him, His face was kind and gentle. When He looks at you, it is like looking into the heart of Yahweh. He seems to see every sin, and every hurt, and every failure. And yet, He loves you, and He forgives you. And He... He harbours nothing against you. It is like He *wants* to forgive you, if only you would just follow Him. He's so full of love and forgiveness, however..." Aunt Rachel looked thoughtful, as she slipped into depths of silence.

After a few moments, Erstis could not hold back any longer. "However?" she prompted her pondering Aunt.

Aunt Rachel startled at the sound of Erstis' voice. "Oh, I'm sorry, dear. I was just remembering something. Where was I? Oh yes, He spoke with authority, like I've never heard before. It was

55

as if the whole earth, and everything in it, somehow... belonged to Him. I know it sounds crazy, but that is how it made me feel."

"I don't believe that's crazy at all, Aunt Rachel. I just wish that I could see Him. So, what happened? Did He teach? Did He perform any miracles? Please don't leave out a single detail!"

"All right. Let me start at the beginning, then. Like I said, Ruth and I were up early. As soon as we heard people walking past, we followed the crowd. I do believe that we had the best spot in the house. We were just inside the door, so we could see Him clearly, and hear all that He said. However, His voice somehow seemed to carry out into the streets, so that everyone could hear Him clearly. We could also see out the door, to the many people that wanted to see Him. It was so crowded that we were all pressed together. Yet, He seemed to see each one of us as individuals. It seemed like He has known me since I was born — but He's younger than me, so that doesn't seem possible."

"Anyway," she continued, shaking her head, "He was visiting with his friends when we all arrived. But He didn't seem to be the least bit upset by our disturbance. He simply raised his head and smiled. His friends were asking Him questions. As He answered them, He would teach some very interesting things. Everything was in accordance with the Scriptures, but His teachings felt more personal.

"I'd always thought that Yahweh was way up in Heaven, and didn't really care about us. I felt like He just gave us a lot of rules to live by — as if He was the judge, sitting up on His throne

56

in Heaven, and we were an army of little ants, doing whatever He had commanded us to do.

"But since hearing this Yeshua speak, I don't think that's the way Yahweh the Father intended it to be. It seems like He really does care for us. He really wants us to have a personal relationship with Him, not just fulfill our religious duties. He wants us to talk to Him, and become... like friends. We are His children. People judge us by what we say and do — they look only at the outside — but Yahweh looks at our hearts.

"Suddenly," she said as she eagerly moved forward in her seat, "my attention was torn away from Him. I heard a commotion outside in the streets. The Pharisees and the teachers of the Law were making their way through the crowd. I think they were upset. They are used to people making way for them, and bowing, calling them "Rabbi" as they pass. Well, yesterday the people were so enthralled by Yeshua, they didn't pay any attention to the Pharisees, except to grumble because they were pushing their way through and disturbing the lesson that Yeshua was teaching.

"Finally," she snickered, "they made it inside the house. They stood in a corner, and listened with critical ears to all that Yeshua was saying. He would often look at them with such an obvious intensity, almost as if He were willing them to listen and understand that Yahweh was not happy with how they have been misleading His children. And yet, He was still willing to forgive them, if they would only confess their sin — similar to what that man in the wilderness preaches... who is he? Oh, yes! John the Baptist, they call him."

"Mmhmmm," nodded Erstis as her aunt continued.

"Then, suddenly, I became aware of another rumpus outside!" Her eyes opened wide. "As I turned around, I noticed that four men carried another man on a stretcher. The crowd reacted differently this time. Nobody would move out of the way at all. People told them they couldn't see Yeshua — they said they would have to wait for another time.

"You remember Jotham, the son of Zerah, who was paralysed in that ploughing accident, back when you were a child? Well, it was his four brothers who carried him on his bedroll. It appeared to me that they were leaving because they couldn't get through.

"I continued listening to Yeshua teaching. There was a feeling of excitement and expectancy in the air. We all were waiting to see Yeshua do another miracle. I don't know how to describe how it felt, except that it seemed as if the power of Yahweh was right there in the room. I could feel it!

"Soon, I heard noises on the roof. I suppose that Jotham's brothers had gone to the back of the house, and climbed up the stairs to the roof. Then they began uncovering the roof! The whole while, Yeshua kept right on speaking, never once being bothered or hindered by the noise or the clumps of falling clay!

"Finally, there was a gap large enough for the bedroll to fit through. The four faithful men had fastened ropes to the bedroll so that they could lower it through the hole in the roof. A hush fell over the crowd in the house as they lowered the paralysed man into the room. The four men peered through the opening as their muscles strained to lower their dear brother carefully and gently. Whispers were passed along to the crowd outside of what was happening. They lowered the bedroll directly in front of Yeshua!

"People pushed back to make room for the Jotham's bedroll to be set down. Yeshua stood and looked at the pitiful form that lay there. You can imagine how much Jotham's legs had withered after all these years. I could tell that Yeshua's gaze pierced into the man's heart. By the look on Jotham's face, I'm sure that he was indeed sorry for every sin he had ever committed.

"Finally, Yeshua spoke to him. He said, 'Son, your sins are forgiven you.' The two men continued looking steadfastly at each other for a few moments. Then..."

Aunt Rachel paused. With a slight shake of her head, she continued. "Then, as if Yeshua had actually heard the thoughts of the Scribes and Pharisees, He looked over at them and said, 'Why are you reasoning in your hearts? Which is easier to say, "Your sins are forgiven you" or to say, "Rise up and walk"? I said it that way so you may know that the Son of Man has power and authority on earth to forgive sins.' Then he looked back to Jotham, and spoke with full authority and love, 'I say to you, arise, take up your bed, and go to your house.'"

Erstis gasped. Her hand flew up to her heart.

Aunt Rachel, encouraged by Erstis' reaction, continued her tale. "Immediately, he stood up before us all! He picked up the bedroll that he had been laying on for so many years, and departed for his own home, glorifying Yahweh all the way!" She flung her hands into the air. "We were all amazed! The power of Yahweh filled the room and the streets outside! We all glorified Yahweh! The crowd parted like the Red Sea. Jotham leaped, ran, and danced all the way home, declaring that the power of Yahweh had touched him.

"Everyone began to disperse, telling all of the strange things that we had seen. Surely, He must be the Son of G-d! For only G-d can perform miracles like that!" finished Aunt Rachel with a wave of her hand for emphasis.

Erstis leaned forward on her seat, and said, "And only Yahweh can forgive sins! He must be the Messiah! Who else could perceive the thoughts of the Pharisees and Scribes?"

"Of course He is the Messiah!" answered Aunt Rachel. "He gives all the glory to Yahweh for everything He has done! Yahweh is the one who gives Him His power! Of course He's the Messiah! I have no doubt whatsoever!"

Hope whispered motivating words into Erstis' soul, which she spoke aloud. "If He is the Messiah, and since He cleansed the leper and healed the paralytic, then He can heal me too!" Unable to contain her enthusiasm, Erstis stood to her feet, holding onto her cushioned seat for added support.

"Oh, Erstis." Aunt Rachel stood and took a step closer, about to put her hand upon Erstis' arm. Suddenly, she remembered the situation, and jerked her hand back. Doubt was hissing words into Aunt Rachel's ear. In turn, she spewed the words out of her mouth. "Oh, honey, you can't go into public! How would you ever get to Him? If someone saw you, you could be stoned! You wouldn't want to risk that, would you? You had better just sit here where you're safe. Maybe we shouldn't bother you with any more stories of the Carpenter..." Aunt Rachel sighed. Her words pierced Erstis' heart like a knife.

Hope lunged at Doubt, slicing his sword through the tip of his black wing.

"Oh, no! I love to hear about what He's doing, and what He's teaching! It's so encouraging! You don't know how depressing it gets, staying here, remembering the doctor's last words. I need something to lift my spirits," begged Erstis.

Hope and Doubt soared high into the sky, duelling with their swords. They left Erstis unattended for the moment.

Aunt Rachel smiled, before turning toward the road out in front of the little hut. "Of course. I'm sorry, honey. Ruth told me that the doctor said it wouldn't be very long now." As she walked, sadness covered her like a cloak and her eyes were downcast. She realized her niece was perilously close to the threshold of death.

Erstis walked with her aunt to the front of the hut, being sure to keep her distance. "Thank you for coming, and for

61

bringing me water, Aunt Rachel. Is Mother coming to deliver milk in two days' time, like usual?"

"Oh, I almost forgot to tell you!" declared Aunt Rachel. "Your Mother has gone to see your Aunt Esther in Gadara. She will be back tomorrow, but will need to rest for a few days. Your sister Hannah will come in two days' time. She'll bring you all the news from Aunt Esther's family. You know that your cousin Damarius is due to be delivered of her first child any day now?"

"Oh, yes!" Erstis replied, "Does she still live near that crazy man in the Gadarenes? You remember, the one who lives in the tombs and screams day and night?"

Aunt Rachel frowned and spoke in low tones, as she looked about. "Yes, that's right. I don't know why they stay there. It's just because that property has been in your Uncle Azor's family for five generations, and he's as stubborn as a bull. He won't give up that land, even to get away from the lunatic!"

"Well, poor Damarius must be having such a trying time," Erstis sympathized with her cousin. "Can you imagine being in the family way, and having to listen to a crazy man crying out like that? They say he screams because he cuts himself with stones."

"I'm sure it's very difficult for Damarius," nodded Aunt Rachel.

"I heard they've tried binding him in chains and shackles, but he breaks them off. I think he must be possessed of a devil. Why else would he act that way?" continued Erstis.

62

"Oh, I don't know. It's not edifying to talk about such things."

"Well, thank you for telling me," said Erstis. "I'll be expecting Hannah. May Yahweh richly bless you, dear Auntie!" She waved farewell to her company.

Erstis turned and walked toward her home. A little, black beast — known as Weakness to those in the spiritual realm — leaped toward her feet. He sank his sharp talons into her ankles, causing her legs to feel heavy and weak. She began to wonder if she would even make it into her small abode. Step after step, Erstis dragged her feet until she finally entered her hut. Groping her way along the wall, she soon flopped down onto her cushion. Taking deep breaths, she squeezed her eyes shut, trying to shut out the feeling of the room reeling around her.

Strength boldly approached her, and spoke softly into her ear. "You need to have some nourishment." Pushing herself up, she made her way to the large jar of milk. Weakness started losing his grip on her ankles. Then, with a burst of determination, he clasped his claws back onto her. As she stumbled across the room, he scrambled along the floor to keep his hold on her.

The warmth of the day had caused the milk to develop a thin layer of scum on top. Without bothering to scrape it off, Erstis filled her mug. Returning to the cushion, she sat calmly and breathed deeply, between sips of the creamy white milk.

"Now," soothed Strength gently, "you also need to strengthen your Spirit." Weakly, Erstis began to hum the Psalms that she knew from her childhood. She always felt the peace of Yahweh when she sang the Psalms.

She remembered the words of a favourite Psalm as she hummed. *The joy of the Lord is my strength.* The more she hummed, the stronger she began to feel. Weakness was losing his hold on her legs.

Unexpectedly, her lips parted and the song burst forth from her heart. "The joy of the Lord is my strength..." Her voice was quiet, but sweet. Weakness's grip loosened even more, but he still tried desperately to hang on, in spite of how much it stung him to hear Erstis calling upon the Name of Yahweh in song.

Out of the blue, Peace swooped into the room. He gave Weakness a swift kick, sending him tumbling across the floor. Desire and Hope joined Strength in attending to Erstis, while Peace rid the house of the pesky demon.

By order of the Master, a heavenly host stood guard around that unclean little hut, keeping evil intruders out of the way. All at once, the angels created an opening where Weakness went flying out of the house. As he flew through the throngs of angelic beings, he was kicked, butted with swords, and hurled off into space.

Inside the hut, Hope, Peace, Strength, and Desire encouraged Erstis, preparing her for a divine appointment.

CHAPTER FOUR

The Sane "Crazy" Man

(Mark 5:1-20)

The sun's rays spread golden fingers brightly across the land. As Erstis lay on her bedroll, she prayed for strength for the day ahead. How she missed the days when she rose up before the sun, worshipping the Lord before starting her day!

Now she lay still, wondering what was going to happen to her in the day ahead. Her sister Hannah was going to bring milk today — but it wasn't just the thought of the creamy milk that caused the stirring of excitement in her heart, nor was it the fact that she would bring news of her Aunt Esther's family.

It was the hope that Hannah would bring more news about Yeshua that caused her heart to race and her face to flush. Unknown to Erstis, Peace was still standing near her bedroll, strengthening her. His massive form overshadowed his tiny charge's shrivelled body. Strength and Hope, however, had gone to meet with the Master in order to receive an update on the situation at hand. Desire — another large being, though not as formidable as Peace — was guarding the door against intruders. Invisible to the human eye, other bright angelic beings were posted all about the front fence, lingering behind trees, standing near the seats out back, and walking through the yard.

Up in the trees, little black leathery beasts rasped out fears and questions about their own mission. How were they to get to Erstis? How could they stop her from going to see Yeshua, the Messiah? To the demons surrounding the hut, the angels portrayed a picture of ignorance. If the dark ones thought that the angels weren't aware of the scouts, they would not be so careful with their next move.

Meanwhile, in the Den of Darkness just outside the city, Schemer and Betrayer were having a discussion with Lucifer, the Father of Lies. A dark cave — not yet discovered by humans — lay hidden behind the rocky ledge of the hills to the south of the city. Roots from the trees above stuck out of the ceiling and wreathed their way along the walls. Moss and long, thin fingers of roots hung down from the thicker roots, which wound and crawled their way along the walls. Had there been a crack to allow any amount of light into the cave, it would have created a frightening picture. The dank odour of mud mixed with stale air created the perfect atmosphere for the demons of darkness to discuss their sinister plot.

Fear, Death, Weakness, Doubt, and Depression were the special delegates brought in to give an account, since they could relate their first hand-experiences. With the exception of Weakness, each of them were massive beings. Each time they succeeded in their tasks, the stronger they became. Weakness was a slithering little demon that made up for his lack of strength by being an expert with his sword. With one quick slice of his blade, his victim would suffer severe pain.

"The heavenly ones have taken guard on the whole yard." stated Death. "There's no way to get to her without fatal consequences to ourselves."

Fear quivered, looking around from side to side. "I'm afraid they outnumber us, Father."

Trembling before the towering Father of Lies, Weakness whined, "They're really big! They're much stronger than we are!"

"Enough!" shouted Lucifer as he pounded his fist on the wall, causing clumps of dirt to fall to the ground. The sound of his voice reverberated throughout the meeting place, causing the demons to cower, lest he take a swipe at them instead of the wall. "Do any of you have any news worth listening to?" The air was thick with silence.

"*WELL*?" he bellowed. Still there was no answer from the quivering group.

"Schemer!" he hollered. The scrawny beast stood to his feet, careful to stay out of reach of the iron fist. "What do we do about this... problem?" asked Lucifer.

Schemer cleared his throat, stalling for time, "Well, it appears, sir, that the best way to handle this is a head-on attack. Leave the special delegates out of it at first. Sending in our strongest warriors first will be enough to capture the attention of their guards. Then, the delegates can swoop in and finish the job."

"Betrayer, will that work?" the huge voice bellowed.

"With all due respect, sir, I don't believe that it would. We cou—"

"Very well, we'll do it!" interrupted the General. He was smart enough to know that if Betrayer disagreed, then it was a plan worth putting into action. "Now, go plan the details! Be off with you!" With a sweep of his hand, the troops dispersed.

The hill above the cave, with its steep rocky ledge, didn't appear to be anything out of the ordinary. However, all at once, it seemed to explode with black slithering beasts emerging from it in every direction. Then, in a cloud of darkness, they were gone. Had anyone been looking at the hill at that moment, they might have noticed a shadow that passed rather quickly over the hill. Within no more than an instant, however, the demons had reassembled in their own meeting area, away from the General.

The sun was already high in the sky. Back at the little hut, Erstis was trying to get out of bed. Every time she moved, the room would start swirling around her head. Then her legs would turn into jelly, and her stomach would start rolling. Sometimes she wondered why she bothered to force milk down her constricted throat, when she would inevitably spew it out. Time and time again, Erstis would go through the endless cycle of trying to drink. Added to the continuous knot of pain that tied itself in her abdomen, it looked as if the doctor's prediction was indeed being fulfilled.

Suddenly, she heard the Voice of Promise softly reminding her, "You have found favour in the eyes of the Lord. Because of your great faith, generation after generation will glorify the Lord G-d of Israel." Erstis sighed and slowly sipped her drink.

Outside Erstis' home, Strength swooped down into an unoccupied tree. He sat on a branch, and assessed the position and strength of the enemy. He only saw half a dozen scouts hiding in the trees by the road, and assumed that the rest of them must be elsewhere making their plans. He would wait for Revealer to meet him — he would know what their plans entailed.

It always amazed the mighty angel that the demons didn't notice Revealer as he silently slipped down through the ground, to rest on the branches in a dark corner of their cave. Surely they must have had some small demons on the lookout for intruders. Strength supposed that they thought heavenly beings were too pure to descend into the evil dungeons.

Suddenly, he became aware of another presence sitting on the branch. Without needing to look beside him to see the little angel, he knew who it was. Outwardly, Revealer appeared to be weak and insignificant, but his ability to blend in and move stealthily was invaluable to the heavenly host. "Well, Revealer, what have you found out?" asked Strength.

The two sat together, as Revealer exposed the plot that was afoot. Then, Strength flew swiftly back to bring an update to the others. They would plan their defence accordingly.

As Erstis finally began her day, she marvelled at the peace of G-d that she felt deep within her heart. She had always worshipped Yahweh by humming or singing the Psalms throughout her day, and even when it seemed that it was time for her to give up and die, she would recall a Psalm that would fill her with peace. As a young girl, she had learned the Scriptures by heart. Mama had felt that it was very important for every Jewish child.

"You can survive without being a good cook or cleaner, but you'll never survive without knowing the Scriptures," Mama would often say.

During the past twelve years, Erstis was grateful beyond measure for her Mama's insistence. She could no longer listen to the Torah being read each Sabbath — only her memory allowed her to recall the beauty of the words. They seemed to nourish her spirit better than fortified milk nourished her body.

She still felt peace within her heart, even as she scooped out her dried herbal powder and noticed that she would only have enough for one more day. When it was gone, she would have to drink plain milk instead. Her money was spent — she had no way to get any more funds.

"How strange," she mused aloud, "after the Doctor's final judgement, I feel more at peace than I've felt all along. It is as if I know that I'm not going to die. My symptoms are growing worse every day — yet sometimes, I feel stronger than I've been in years." She paused to think for a moment.

But the strangest thing is how quiet the town has been. Yeshua must have left town for a while.

As she puttered about her little room, sipping her drink, she remembered the days that she and Hannah had spent together growing up. *What blissful days they were, not having any cares or worries. Now Hannah's busy tending to her family. I've heard that her husband is a wonderful man.*

She remembered the day when Hannah brought her son Uzziah to the gate, so that she could see him from a distance. Erstis did not go close to him, for fear that he may contract something dreadful from her. Erstis sighed. *What a precious boy...*

Just then, she heard her sister's voice outside. "Erstis! Your sister Hannah is here! Come out and meet me!"

Unknown to Erstis or Hannah, Strength and Hope walked alongside Hannah. As they walked, they assessed the enemy surrounding the hut. As of yet, no move had been made to increase the number of demons that were milling about. They would come soon enough. But the Master had sent in a hundred sentries, two by two, who were hiding until the attack came.

Erstis and Hannah went through the usual ritual of exchanging greetings, then pouring the milk into the clay jar, always mindful that Hannah not touch anything that Erstis had touched, lest she become unclean also.

As they strolled slowly to the back yard, Peace, Strength, and Hope stood guard close enough to protect them if the need should arise — yet they did not interfere with the conversation.

"How is cousin Ruth feeling?" Erstis asked.

"Oh, she's perky as ever!" replied Hannah, as she seated herself in the cushioned seat intended for visitors. "She's drawing near to her confinement time. I think she'll visit you once more before she is delivered of the babe."

"That's wonderful!" exalted Erstis.

Before she could go on, Hannah leaned forward with a mischievous gleam in her eye. "Guess who I saw at the market?"

Hannah often played the "guess who" game with Erstis, so that she wouldn't feel left out of town life.

"Was it cousin Jonas?" asked Erstis, playing along with her sister. A smile spread across her face.

"No, sister! Someone much more handsome... Moshe!"

At the sound of his name, Erstis pictured his charming smile and the dimple in his left cheek. She remembered how a lock of his hair would always fall over his left eye and he would push it aside, not realizing how the motion caused the muscles in his arms to ripple. She slowly sucked in her breath as her heart wreathed in pain, at the mention of her true love.

She remembered that Hannah had liked Moshe, too. Of course she would — all the girls could see how handsome and charming he was. But Moshe only had eyes for Erstis.

"How is he?" she asked, her eyes downcast.

"Oh, he's as wonderful as ever!" Hannah extolled. "He asked about you. Did you know that he never married?" She flung her hands about as she spoke. She always seemed to be moving even when she was sitting.

"Yes." Erstis said wistfully. "He told me that he would never marry anyone else. He said that he would wait for me to get better." She tilted her head to look at the rocky cliff. "We didn't know that it would take so long."

Her mind wandered back once again to that last special day. Moshe was something of a rascal. They had hugged, and even kissed on the lips. Erstis sighed as she imagined the feeling of his lips on hers.

Hannah's mischievous attitude changed to one of solemnity, as she realized that she had brought her sister grief instead of joy. Putting on a wobbly smile, she tried to sound positive. "Well, it won't be long now, and you'll be better. Then you'll be married to Moshe."

Erstis slowly turned and looked at her sister. With pity she said, "Hannah, I know that it's hard for you to accept — the fact that your sister is dying."

Hannah's hand went up to her mouth. She sucked in a sob, shaking her head in denial as tears filled her eyes and threatened to spill down her cheeks.

"It's true, Hannah. The doctor said that it won't be much longer now. In fact, I thought that I might have gone two days

75

ago, but I cried out to Yahweh. He gave me strength to continue on. I've been feeling such amazing peace. Now, sister, dry your tears, and let's enjoy our visit together. Please tell me, has cousin Damarius brought forth her child? Please tell me all about Mama's visit."

Erstis leaned back in her seat to listen to the story of her mother's visit with her relatives. Hannah sniffed and dried her tears on her beautifully hand-embroidered handkerchief. Erstis remembered when Mama had taught her and Hannah how to do fine needlepoint. She had just started creating her own patterns before she got sick. She was sure that she could have brought in some extra income for herself and Moshe by selling her work. She had already saved up quite a bit by selling them. Now, all of her money had been spent on doctors and medicine.

Bringing her attention back to Hannah, she noticed that her sister had regained control of her emotions and was beginning to relate the story of their Mama's visit.

"Oh..." began Hannah, rather hesitantly. "She had a very, ah... interesting visit. Cousin Damarius bore a healthy boy child! They are all very pleased! Mama says that Aunt Esther's face shone like the sun!"

"Praise be to Yahweh!" rejoiced Erstis, as she raised her hands to glorify G-d. At her quick movement, however, her head began to spin. She leaned forward and rested her head in her hands.

Instantly, Hannah reached toward Erstis, but then came to a sudden halt. She was only a hand's length away from touching her unclean sister. "Are you all right? What's the matter?" She knew her sister longed to soothe her, but had held back because of the law's restrictions.

Strength stood nearby, watching with longing. He had been given orders that he couldn't offer any more strength to Erstis. The time had come for her to go through the next fiery trial — on her own. Strength would need to fight the dark demons when they attacked. Hope, however, stood close to Erstis, and spoke secretly to her. "This too shall pass. Take deep breaths."

"I-I-I'm... fine," gasped Erstis weakly. "Just... let this weak spell... pass." She rested her head in her hands, trying to breathe deeply.

Hannah was obviously shaken by her sister's sudden weakness. Erstis could see that it caused Hannah to realize that her long struggle was really coming to an end. Death could take her any day now.

With another deep breath, Erstis finally sat up, leaning her head back. "Please... tell me... is there any news... about... Yeshua... the Nazarene?"

"Well," began Hannah, as she glanced around her, making sure that nobody was near. "Aunt Rachel said that I wasn't to fill your mind with ideas that might get you into trouble, but if—"

77

"Oh, please tell me! I'm so weak... but I'm trying to keep the faith. It encourages me to hear... how He heals people... and does miracles." Erstis slowly regained strength as she continued to inhale and exhale deeply. She held her head up, and gave her sister a feeble smile.

At her sister's continued reluctance, she said in a pleading voice, "Please, Hannah, don't rob me of the only pleasure that I can enjoy... while I still can..." She looked up at her sister, her eyes urging her to share the story.

"Oh, Erstis," she soothed, "you know that I could never deny you anything. Now, I'll tell you what happened, if you'll put your head back and relax."

Erstis smiled and lay her head back, gratefully closing her eyes. As Hannah related the intriguing story, Erstis imagined it, as if she were watching a play unfold right before her eyes.

"Well, mother was having tea with Aunt Esther one afternoon, when suddenly, they heard screeching and screaming. A few minutes later they heard a loud, thundering noise and pigs squealing. Then it stopped. There was an eerie silence."

Erstis eyes opened wide. She couldn't keep her eyes closed any longer. She sat straight up in her seat and asked, "Really? Did they find out what it was all about?"

"Yes, they did. Only a few minutes later, our young cousin Abuid came rushing in. He helps his friends tend their herd

NAMELESS A Story of Faith

of about two thousand swine. They saw the whole thing and told Mama and Aunt Esther what happened.

"They said they were in the hills watching the herd when they saw Yeshua and his disciples come across the lake in a boat to the Gadarenes. While they were still a long way off, that crazy man that lives in the tombs started shrieking worse than ever!

"He ran to Yeshua, shouting at Him. He called Him the Son of G-d! He asked why He was interfering with him. Then he begged him not to torture him!"

"Torture him?" asked Erstis. "I thought Yeshua was a gentle and loving man. He wouldn't torture him, would he?"

"Well, it turns out the crazy man was possessed by demons, and it was the devils inside him that were talking. Yeshua had already told the spirit to come out of him. So, it was the demon asking Yeshua not to torture him."

"Ohhh..." breathed Erstis.

"Yes! Then Yeshua demanded him to tell Him what his name was. He said it was 'Legion' because they were many. Can you imagine? The man was possessed by *many* devils! No wonder he was so crazy! Then Yeshua commanded them to come out of the man. They begged Him again and again not to send them out of the region. By this time, Abuid and his friends had come closer so they could hear and see everything very clearly. The devils inside the man asked Him to send them into the herd of pigs on the hill. Then, Yeshua commanded 'Go!' And you'll never believe what happened then!"

"What happened?" she asked eagerly.

"The demons went into the swine and the entire herd went mad! They began squealing and stampeding. They rushed right over the cliff and plunged into the river! Every one of the pigs drowned!"

Hope, still standing near Erstis, leaned in closer and whispered thoughts to her. She spoke the thoughts out loud. "Oh, Father Yahweh!" exclaimed Erstis. "He must be the Messiah! He has power over demons! And He has power to forgive sins, and to heal the sick!"

"That's not all! Abuid's friends were angry about losing their whole herd. They got all the men from the town together to go out and talk to Yeshua, but nobody could have guessed what they found when they got there."

"What did they find?"

"That crazy, demon-possessed man was sitting there fully clothed and perfectly sane!"

"What? He was sane? How could that be?" Erstis wondered.

"Well," Hannah continued, "obviously he had been made crazy by the legion of devils that possessed him. Once Yeshua had delivered him from the demons, he wasn't crazy anymore."

"Everyone in the town was spooked! They started pleading with Yeshua to leave them alone. Yeshua and His disciples were getting back into the boat to leave when Abuid heard the crazy man — who is now sane — begging to go with Him. Then he heard Yeshua tell him to go home to his family, and tell everyone all that Yahweh has done for him."

Erstis couldn't contain her excitement. "Wow! This man Yeshua must really be the Messiah! Don't you see? He has been healing sick people and casting out demons. If He's done that for them, why couldn't He do that for me, too?"

Hannah looked at her uncomfortably. "Erstis, honey, please don't get so excited. I'm sure it's not good for you. Besides..." she looked about her again, as if she expected to see her Aunt Rachel or Cousin Ruth hiding nearby, eavesdropping on their conversation. "A-Aunt R-Rachel said that I wasn't supposed to talk to you about Yeshua." She knew that their Mama would not be too happy, either.

"And why not?" Erstis rallied. "It's bad enough that I'm confined to this place and cannot see Him. Would you also deny me the pleasure of hearing about Him?"

"Erstis, please don't get so upset. If you're going to continue, I'll have no choice but to leave." Her face was that of a brave warrior. As much as she wanted to tell her sister about

81

Yeshua the Carpenter, she didn't want to cause more problems. "Besides," she had lamented on her way to the visit, "I will not be the one to get Erstis upset, and cause her death."

Erstis took a deep breath as she focused on her view of the hill, remembering that her strength comes from the Lord. Hope spoke to her once again. "You can be healed! He wants to heal you, too!"

Leaning forward, Erstis rested her arms on her lap and looked intently into her sister's dark eyes. Hannah started to squirm under the scrutinizing gaze. Finally, Erstis spoke. "Hannah, tell me... do you know that I am about to die?"

Hannah looked away, her eyes downcast. She sucked in her breath as she brought her fist up to her mouth, and began to gently bite on her finger. She had a habit of doing so whenever she was upset.

"Now, sister. Surely you have heard that this Yeshua has healed the leper, and He also healed Jotham, the lame man," continued Erstis.

Her sister, looking off into the distance, continued to bite idly at her own fist.

"Now, Hannah," Erstis said calmly but sternly, "tell me truthfully. Would you not want me to be healed, so that I can hug you once again? I could greet you with the holy kiss and..." Erstis paused until Hannah lifted her gaze and looked into her sister's wistful eyes. "... and I could marry Moshe, and have children!"

Her voice had grown in intensity until she hurled the last two words at Hannah, with a fling of her hands, as if she were placing her destiny in her sister's hands.

Hannah leaned forward in her seat, before addressing her sister in a soothing tone of voice. "Erstis, of course I want that for you. But what I do not want..." she paused, before articulating each of her next words clearly, with emphasis. "What I do not want is for you to go outside the gate and end up being stoned to death! You know that you're not permitted to mingle with the public."

"Hannah, do you not think that Yahweh would keep me protected from harm when I'm stepping out in faith?" demanded Erstis. Hope was taking advantage of the fact that Doubt was preoccupied with the planning session with his cohorts. He used the chance to fill Erstis with greater optimism than ever.

Faith made a swooshing entrance onto the scene. He was a massive being with firm, muscular arms and legs, and He towered above the other angels. His blonde hair and golden skin gave him the appearance of a Greek god.

The command had come forth. Erstis was ready for Faith to help her in the battle. The enemy was so engrossed in their own planning that they had failed to take note of the enormous angelic entrance. Had they known, they would have trembled, for Faith imparted the ability to make the impossible possible.

"Faith," Erstis continued, "doesn't do much good, unless I put some action with it. That's when you really believe! You see,

83

Hannah, if you really believe that Yeshua is the Messiah, then you would take me to see Him, like Jotham's brothers took him. Now *they* had faith!"

Hannah jerked back, as if Erstis had slapped her. She sucked in her breath sharply. "Well! I can't believe that you would say those things — that I don't have faith!"

Faith came close beside Erstis and began to speak to her. In turn, she in spoke his words to her sister.

"Hannah," Erstis said soothingly as she leaned toward her sister, "I don't mean to be cruel. I just need you to understand. It feels like my soul is crying out to be free from this disease and uncleanness. And I feel like He is listening. It's like He can hear me and He wants me to exercise my faith by going to Him, so that He can heal me. I feel like He is calling me to come to Him. I know it sounds strange, but that is how I feel."

"Erstis," Hannah sighed, "I don't pretend to know, let alone understand, how you must feel. But I do know that I love you, and I don't want you to get hurt. Surely, you must know that as soon as you meet someone on the street, they will know that you are sick and unclean. You won't even get a chance to reach Yeshua! They'll stone you in the street!"

Doubt had known the day before that he would be called away. Therefore, to retain a foothold in Erstis' life, he had used their Mama and their aunt to fill Hannah's mind with skepticism. Now, even though he wasn't with her, she remembered the words of Mama and Aunt Rachel. She was filled with doubt.

"Well, I can see that you aren't going to support me, either." Erstis sat back in her chair. Her voice was not angry, merely disappointed. "I always thought I could count on you."

"Erstis, you can depend on me," retorted Hannah. "You can depend on me to stand up for what is best for you. That's what you can depend on!"

With a sigh, Erstis said softly, "Thank you, Hannah. I do know that you love me. And I know that you want what is best for me. You have been a wonderful sister, and I love you dearly. Now, sister, I am getting weary. If you'll kindly forgive me, I'll go and lie down to get some rest." Weakly, Erstis pushed herself up off of the chair.

Hannah stood as well. "Sure, honey. I'm sorry. I shouldn't have upset you, and I shouldn't have stayed so long. Please, forgive me." As they walked back to the hut, Hannah stretched out her hand toward Erstis. Barely a finger's breadth away from touching her, she stopped.

Both women jerked their hands apart. They paused in shock at what had just transpired, and what the effects could have been. Slowly, they both turned and walked toward the front gate together, as Erstis whispered, "You're forgiven."

At the door to the hut, Hannah turned and softly said, "Get some rest, dear."

Erstis smiled and ducked into her little house. As Hannah reached the front gate, she realized that she hadn't mentioned that

Mama would be by in two days with some fresh water. She turned to tell Erstis, but she had already gone inside. Hannah sighed and continued on her way, hoping that Erstis would figure it out on her own.

Inside the little house, Erstis fell to her knees and cried out to Yahweh in a Psalm.

"Oh Lord my Yahweh, in You I put my trust;

Save me from all those who persecute me;

And deliver me,

Lest they tear me like a lion,

Rending me in pieces, while there is none to deliver.

O Lord my Yahweh if I have done this:

If there is iniquity in my hands,

If I have repaid evil to him who was at peace with me,

Or have plundered my enemy without cause,

Let the enemy pursue me and overtake me;

Yes, let him trample my life to the earth,

86

And lay my honour in the dust.

Selah...

...I will praise the Lord according to His righteousness,

And will sing praise to the name of the Lord Most High."[10]

With Peace, Hope, Strength, and Faith all guarding her, Erstis climbed into her bedroll for a much-needed long and peaceful rest.

CHAPTER FIVE

It's for me!

(Luke 8:40 - 42)

Erstis had been sleeping peacefully since the previous afternoon. Although she was unaware of it, heavenly forces protected her while she slept. Hundreds of reinforcements had been sent in by the Master. They were hiding anywhere they could — all about the yard, in trees, and behind rocks and furniture. Only the usual angels were out in the open. Their strategy was to let the host of darkness think that the heavenly host was unaware of their scheme. Some of the evil scouts had reported that they had seen newcomers, but they had no idea how many there were.

Erstis rested very deeply until just before sunrise. In the pre-dawn light, dark shadows stole through the streets and floated into town. They all headed toward the little hut on the outskirts of town, nestled beneath the high rock cliff.

As the angels unsheathed their swords from their scabbards in unison, the resounding ring of metal throughout the yard was unheard by humans. Muscles tensed and rippled as the angels stood at attention, and even the hidden angels held their swords in anticipation. They were on guard, ready to pounce on any little demon that passed by.

As the enemy host slithered in from the streets, the angels that were out in the open fought to keep them at bay. The cloud of darkness descended upon them. One by one the secluded angels leapt on the unsuspecting demons.

Faith, Peace, and Strength ministered to Erstis while she rested. She needed the long, peaceful rest to prepare for the lengthy battle ahead. Hope and Desire stood guard outside. They fought away any pesky little beasts that had made their way through the ring of angels encircling Erstis' humble dwelling-place.

High in a tree near the rear of the house, Revealer sat as still as a stone. From his clever perch he could clearly see all throughout the yard, and he could see the close-knit fence of angels around the cottage. He paid particular attention to Hope and Desire swooping around between the hut and the angelic fence, keeping out any demons that made their way through.

The only part of Revealer that moved was his eyes. He surveyed the battle from east to west, north to south, his eyes swaying from one direction to another. He looked up into the sky, then down to the ground.

Finally, he saw a dark cloud moving in over on the western horizon. "So," he thought, "the delegates are on their way." Like a bullet, he shot out of the tree with his sword pointed straight out in front of him, flying across the yard and through the walls of the hut. Any demons in his path were sliced right through. Amazingly, no angels were caught in his path.

Once inside, Revealer enlightened the three guardians about the incoming demonic force. They thanked him and took up their places of protection. Revealer leaped up through the roof to join those who were protecting the hut from above.

When the ones that remained in hiding saw his signal, they darted to the roof like a hundred arrows flying toward one target. Their onslaught of bright arrows slashed through many demons.

Within moments, they joined the angelic fence to form a dome over the hut. Revealer flew high up into the sky to see how close the dark cloud had progressed. The enemy's forces were indeed coming very quickly.

A stream of enemy bandits followed Revealer, forming a long black tail behind him. He led them in a high arc through the sky, and then dove toward the ground. Only a foot from the ground, he arced back toward the heavens. As he glanced quickly behind himself, he noticed that there were a few dim-witted ones that collided with the surface of the earth before they could arc upwards. All that remained of them was a pile of debris on the ground.

Revealer sped up, forcing his demonic followers to travel at an incredible pace to keep up with him. He spurred ahead, flying half a mile into the sky. Then, with a flash of light, he turned sharply in the opposite direction. The point of his sword led the way. He dove straight through the tail of attackers, catching them off guard. Bits and pieces of demons flew to either side, and a rotten stream of greenish-black smoke trailed behind them as they fell.

In a flash, Revealer was back inside the hut once more. He informed the other angels that the cloud would descend upon them in a moment. Erstis began to stir in her sleep, unconsciously sensing the demonic presence approach. The angelic guard tensed and flexed their hands on their swords. They were ready for the attack. Revealer slipped out to join Desire and Hope, who were standing guard outside.

Each angel prayed for Erstis to make it through the coming onslaught. Peace and Strength stood close to her bed, whispering encouraging thoughts to her in her sleep. She began to relax and breathe easily once more.

Just then, Schemer — the sneaky lizard-like devil — broke through the dome of angels and into the small room. Faith immediately raised his sword and took a quick swipe at him. The weaselly thing squirmed out of the way, missing the blow altogether, and caught the angels off guard.

At that precise time, Betrayer broke through the wall, knocking Faith off his feet. Strength leaped after Betrayer. Schemer dashed over to Erstis, taking a swipe at Peace at the same time. Duelling with one hand, he sunk the sharp talons of his other hand deep into her skull, transferring evil thoughts into her mind.

"Your whole family is scheming against you. They're giving you false hope. This Yeshua doesn't do all they say. They're just feeding you a story."

Erstis tossed and turned in her sleep. Faith leaped up off the floor and sped over to Schemer, hitting him with such force that he flew right through the wall and landed outside at Hope's feet. When the slithering trouble-maker saw who stood over him, he whined and took off before Hope had a chance to attack him. He flew through the dome of angels and all the way back to the dungeons, to tend to his wounds.

Just as soon as Schemer left, Doubt came bolting in. He headed straight at Strength, who was holding Betrayer at bay. He slammed into him, sending him sprawling across the floor, unconscious.

Peace was standing by Erstis' side. Betrayer leaped at him, just as Depression entered the hut. Each demon that came was bigger and stronger than the one before it. Now Faith took over guarding the girl, while Peace and Strength fought the newly-arrived demons. When Strength had recovered from his blow to the head, the angels formed a line. The next demon that entered would first be fought by Peace, and then passed on to Strength to wear him out. Then, if the demons didn't flee first, Faith booted them outside, where Hope, Desire, and Revealer tackled them and finished them off.

As the three interior guards shuffled into position, Betrayer had somehow been overlooked. Instantly he sunk both of his taloned hands into Erstis' small skull, attaching his thoughts to

93

hers. "Your family has betrayed you! They should be taking you to Yeshua. The truth is that they know He'll never heal you. They want you to die!"

Erstis let out a moan as she tossed her head from one side to the other. Her moan caught Faith's attention. With a powerful swing of his sword, he pushed Betrayer to the outside guard, where he would be disposed of.

Weakness — a wimpy little devil — entered the hut, taking in the situation at hand. Peace took a swipe at him, while Depression moved on to battle Strength. Faith stood ready to attack Doubt. The sneaky demon drew his opponent to the left, then to the right. Faith lunged to the left to stop the attack, but instead Doubt swooped down. He grabbed Faith by the ankles, and pulled Faith's feet out from under him. Faith landed flat on his back, and was momentarily stunned.

Doubt took advantage of the opportunity. With a quick move, he stabbed at Erstis' stomach. In her sleep, she felt a sharp pain in her lower abdomen. She sucked in her breath, and tossed and turned again. Subconsciously, she heard a deep, resonant voice whisper to her, "Don't believe all the lies your family is telling you. I doubt there even is a Yeshua. And if there is, I truly doubt that he'll heal you. He'll probably throw the first rock to stone you to death."

Strength left Depression stunned for a moment. He took a swipe at Doubt — a deep gash that sliced into the back of his arm. At that moment, Faith came back to escort Doubt to the outside guards. Depression shook his head. He lunged at Faith, but Faith butted him with his sword.

Strength took a swipe at Weakness, but Weakness flipped out of the way. Erstis shivered as Fear entered the room, knocking Peace into a corner as he did so. Strength was then battling both Fear and Weakness at the same time.

As Faith tried to take a swipe at Weakness, Depression conked him on the head. Then, both Depression and Weakness dove towards their innocent victim. Erstis laid on her bedroll in a restless sleep, dreaming of black beasts with scaly wings fluttering about her head, muttering oaths. "You have no strength left," the demons told her. "You're going to die. You'll never make it to Yeshua. He would only curse you if you could go — but you can't! You're too weak! There is no use trying anymore. Just give up!"

In her sleep, her breathing became short and shallow. Her body was so weak that she couldn't even toss and turn any more. She moaned.

Faith and Peace roused at the same time. They tackled Depression and Weakness, sending them tumbling outside. Faith and Peace turned to join Strength in his battle against Fear. They were caught mid-turn by the hulking presence of Death. Death used both fists, each one slamming against one of the angels' smooth faces. Faith and Peace flipped backwards through the air.

Death came up behind Strength and knocked him on the head. As Strength sailed through the air to escape, he also noticed

Peace and Faith lying on the floor. He tried to send the signal to the outside guards to take over, but he sank into unconsciousness before he could manage to call to them.

Fear and Death closed in on Erstis. Her body trembled with Fear as he shouted, "You're going to die! The devil is going to get your soul!"

The Father commanded the outer guards to go in. As the three outer guards leaped to get Death off of her, Fear met them head-on. He sent them sprawling on the floor. Fear stood over them, allowing Death to finish the job.

Death placed his thick talons around Erstis' thin neck. As he started to squeeze, she began choke in her sleep. She dreamed she was being strangled by a faceless man dressed in a black cloak. She could feel Death's fiery breath stinging her face. She gasped weakly, "Abba[11]... Yahweh!"

At her cry, Death began to quiver. He looked all around the little room, he hoped the Master didn't hear her cry.

Suddenly, Death froze in terror as he heard the sound of a mighty rushing wind. That sound could only mean one thing. His most hated enemy was here — Life!

A bright light sliced through the roof of the little house. As Life entered the room with the glory of the Father upon him, his massive figure towered over Death. Fear quivered as he sheepishly looked up at Life, before slinking into a dark corner. The three outside guards regained consciousness, and

96

immediately saw their opportunity. They leaped on Fear. Swords slashed and sliced, sending putrid green smoke into the air.

Death snatched his claws from Erstis and grabbed for His sword. Erstis lay lifeless on the bed.

"So," thundered Death, as he stood to his full height, "we meet again."

"Are you having a problem with your ears?" Life asked in clear, melodic tones.

As Death frowned in confusion, Life started walking closer to Erstis. "Didn't you hear her? She cried out to the Father. That means that *you*," he said as he pointed his finger into Death's chest, "must take your filthy hands off her — and keep them off!"

By then, Death could feel Life's cool, refreshing breath on his face. It repulsed him. He began to cower slightly, but gestured toward the still form and taunted Life. "I've already killed her. What are you going to do now?"

"First," Life said, filled with controlled anger and authority, "I'm going to deal with the filthy little murderer in front of me." Death backed up farther and farther with each step that Life took toward him.

"Then..." he paused dramatically as he leaned down into the face of Death, "I'm going to breathe Life into her."

With a ring of metal, Life unsheathed his sharp sword from its scabbard. Before Death could make a move, Life sliced open his arm, spilling forth a gut-wrenching odour of death and blood.

Death brought his sword up in a stabbing motion toward Life's chest. With a ringing sound, it came to a halt. Death jerked his head to see who was holding the sword that had saved his enemy's life.

Strength smiled at him in victory. Death turned his head to the other side. There he saw Peace and Faith, slowly and decisively bringing the point of their sword to push Death's sword away from Life. Behind them, in a semicircle, Revealer, Desire, and Hope stood on guard.

Death's eyes were wide as they darted in horror from side to side. In an instant, he leaped backward and took a huge arcing sweep with his sword. Peace was caught unaware. Death's sword sliced his thigh.

Faith jumped out of the way, barely avoiding a nick in the forearm. By the time the sword reached Life, he was holding his sword out in front of him for protection.

Life stepped on Death's scaly foot. The point of his sword pierced the outer layers of Death's neck. In an authoritative tone, Life said, "Soon, Yeshua is going to heal her! Now, leave her alone, and don't come back!"

With that declaration, Life raised a muscular arm and sent Death flying backward, out through the wall of the hut. When the remaining demons outside saw that Death had been defeated, they turned around and slinked off to meet the others.

The Father had given Life the command to restore Erstis. Life, empowered by the glory of Yahweh, filled the hut with a blinding light. He went over to the bed where her still form lay. The other angels joined him in a circle about the bed. "There is still some life in her," stated Life.

The entire room blazed with the glory of Yahweh. Life breathed into Erstis, then Strength attended to her. Soon her breathing was regulated. Each angel took their turn ministering to her in their own special way. His work then finished, Life returned to the Father.

As the first fingers of dawn felt their way across the land, Erstis began to stir from her sleep. While she lay there resting, images of her dreams came back to her. Strangely enough, she didn't feel fearful anymore. Indeed, she felt quite peaceful.

Her thoughts drifted to Yeshua of Nazareth. Although Erstis was unaware of it, Faith whispered to her, "All you have to do is go to Yeshua."

Erstis thought for a moment. She opened her eyes widely. Finally she resolved aloud, "I *will* go to Yeshua. And Yeshua *will* heal me!"

She climbed out of bed and filled her mug with milk. She dressed herself, and then purposefully walked out behind her hut. The crisp morning air stung her cheeks, giving them a rosy glow. She remembered when she used to watch the sunrise as a girl. At that time, more than any other, she always felt closer to Yahweh.

On this nippy morning, the Father painted the sky in beautiful crimsons, purples, and pinks. Erstis worshipped Yahweh in Psalms for a few minutes, then asked for wisdom to know what Yahweh willed her to do.

Questions ran through her head, but each question was directly followed by the answer.

All I have to do is find a way to get to Yeshua. I know that He'll have compassion, and will heal me.

"Now," she said aloud, "how am I going to get to Yeshua without being noticed?"

Immediately the answer came: *Wear your black mourning gown with the thick black veil. Wear your black lacy gloves, too, and nobody will notice how white your skin is.*

"Yes," she said as excitedly as the gnawing pain in her stomach would allow. Mama and Papa had provided well for her. What would she have done without them? When they had first realized that this was going to be a long illness, they had given her a beautiful black mourning gown, complete with a lacy veil and gloves to match.

100

"Bless Mama and Papa," she whispered.

Suddenly, her breath caught in her throat.

But what if someone should recognize me? Surely, they would realize that I'm ceremonially unclean. I can't let anyone know who I am. If they recognize me, I could be stoned to death before I reach Yeshua. She picked up a metal bowl and looked at it to get a distorted glimpse of her face. Sad black eyes stared back at her.

Instantly, it struck her that the veil was thick enough that nobody would be able to make out her features. *Even if they did catch a glimpse of me, they wouldn't recognize me. I have lost so much weight that I don't even look like the same person I was twelve years ago.*

"That's right. So, when I get to Yeshua..." Her voice trailed off as she pondered what she would do once she reached Yeshua. *Should I tell Him all about my problems, and how dreadful life has been to one so young? Then everyone in the crowd would pity me... or they may stone me.*

"Well, it doesn't matter," she said, standing to her feet, "I'm going to go inside and find that black outfit. I will be ready when He comes back into town."

The sun had burst over the horizon, and was now shining gloriously. Erstis was thrilled as she walked back to her hut. She muttered to herself, "I'm going to see Yeshua. He's going to heal me. Healing is for me, too."

101

She went inside to set out the black dress and gloves. As she sat on her bedroll, fingering the lace of the veil, she heard shouting. She went to the door, and looked outside.

Men and women were hurrying toward the town centre. They called out to their neighbours as they passed by, "He's coming! The Nazarene Carpenter is coming! Hurry!"

"Oh," Erstis gasped, coming back into the house, "He's here! Today is the day I'm going to see Yeshua!"

Moving as quickly as she possibly could, she donned the black dress, gloves, and veil. Her hands trembled with excitement and nervousness. She fumbled to get the veil in place. It was important that none of her skin be visible.

By the time she was ready, the street was empty. Her heart still pounding, she quickly pattered out to the front yard, but as her hand reached out to push the gate open, Weakness dove straight toward her. He had been concealed in the green leaves of the old tree that was rooted beside the fence.

Weakness sunk his sword deep into Erstis' abdomen, causing her to clutch her stomach and double over in pain.

"Father Yahweh!" she moaned. "I need your strength!" At her cry, Strength swooped in. He brought his sword up, right underneath Weakness' sword. It came dislodged from Erstis' stomach. The two spiritual beings sailed high into the air, clanging their swords in a duel.

Breathing heavily, Erstis gathered her black shawl about her. "I'm not going to think about the doctor's report. I'm just going to focus on how great I felt when I was young."

She made sure the veil fully covered her. With great determination, she reached out her hand to the gate. She took a deep breath. *Once I touch the gate, there's no turning back. I haven't been past the gate in twelve long years!* She pushed open the gate, letting her hand linger on the rough wood as she closed it slowly behind her.

A flood of emotion came over her. For the first thirteen years of her life, she had opened gates every day without a thought. *Now, because of my actions, the fence will have to be burned. It is unclean. But that's okay. I'm going to be healed today! The whole hut will be burned! What a celebration we will have!*

Closing the gate, she looked about to be sure nobody saw her. As quickly as she could, she walked in the direction the crowd had gone.

Doubt flew close and whispered into her ear. "You can't be here! Somebody saw you. You'd better run back, and hide in your bed. You can say that you've been sick in bed all day! They'll believe you, because you're going to die soon anyway."

"No!" She said aloud, as Hope took a swipe at Doubt, "I will not go back. And I will not die!"

She marched into town with fervour, determined to ignore the gnawing pain in her stomach. She held her head high and her shoulders back. She hoped that she would remember the way. It had been such a long time since she had walked these streets.

When she came to the fork in the road, she stopped and listened for some indication as to which way she should go. She could hear people walking down the main street toward the east. Suddenly, she remembered the shortcut that she and Hannah had discovered years ago. At best she would come out ahead of the crowd, but at the very least she would catch up to them.

Appearing to be a young girl in mourning, she moved unhindered through the side streets. Faith, Peace, and Hope moved with her — Faith and Hope on either side of her, and Peace moving ahead of her, in case any demon decided to try a head-on attack.

I must move quickly. I don't want to miss Him.

"My legs feel like lead," she moaned, but she pushed herself forward.

Moments later, the world began to spin around her. She slowed down and came to a stop. She breathed deeply and prayed, "Abba, please give me strength."

Unknown to her, Strength and Weakness still duelled above her. Every now and then, Weakness would dive down and take a stab at her, and either Faith or Hope would try to knock his sword away from her, but occasionally the tip would momentarily pierce her body.

After a few deep breaths, she started walking again. Finally, she made the last turn of the shortcut. There, at the crossing of the main street, was a river of people all flowing in one direction.

If I can get close enough, I can ask somebody where Yeshua is headed. Then maybe I can get there faster by taking another shortcut. The adrenaline was rushing through her body at the thought of joining a public crowd.

The closer she got to the current of people, the faster her heart raced. She felt that she would be swept away with them. Doubt swooped in from behind to say, "You can't go near those people! They'll know! You'll be stoned before you even get near Yeshua! And He won't be able to help you anyway."

Hope brought his elbow up in a quick movement, making instant connection with Doubt's face. Erstis didn't let doubting thoughts slow her one bit. She had her mind made up.

I believe that Yeshua is the Messiah! I believe He has the power to heal me. I even believe He knows about me, and can hear my heart's cry.

Approaching the edge of the crowd, she tried to get someone's attention. "Excuse me, Miss! Excuse me, Sir!"

105

Tammy Leigh Robinson

After trying several times, she finally reached out and took someone by the arm. The young woman's momentum carried Erstis a few steps, until the woman slowed down and turned to look at her, "What do you—"

Erstis cut her off. "Please! Can you tell me where Yeshua is going?" Suddenly, Erstis recognized her as one of the young women she had known when she was a girl.

She ignored Doubt when he shouted at her, "You know her! She'll recognize you! You can't touch her! You'll give her your disease!"

"Don't you know?" asked the young woman, "Oh, of course you don't. You've been in mourning. I'm sorry." She linked her arm through Erstis' arm, and they walked on together.

The young woman continued walking and talking, but Erstis was busy trying to rein in her runaway emotions. The tenderness, love, and acceptance that permeated from her touch were what she had been dreaming of for twelve long years. Not only had Erstis touched this woman, but she had returned her touch. She wanted to hug the woman, but at the same time also wanted to run away.

Finally, she started hearing the words that were being spoken to her, "...the Ruler of the Synagogue. Oh, maybe you're not from this town. Well, his name is Jarius. Anyway..." she rattled on, "his young daughter, an only child, lies on her death bed — even now! So, if we hurry, we can see Yeshua perform a miracle and heal her!"

106

"Where does this man live?" asked Erstis, remembering where he had lived when she was a child. Sure enough, the young woman verified that he was at the same place.

"Thank you. Shalom, my friend." She gave the woman's arm a gentle squeeze, and broke away from her.

Wonderful, thought Erstis, as she made her way back to the edge of the crowd, *I remember just where he lives. I'll be able to cut through, and wait for them near the sandlemaker's. Then I can get to Yeshua.*

She made a quick turn into the next alley. The woman's words raced through her mind. *Yeshua is here! A little girl is dying. He is in a hurry to reach her before she dies.*

Once again, Doubt filled her mind with his inaudible words. "He's on his way to see a dying girl. If you take up His time, she will surely die. It will be your fault! Her blood will be on your unclean hands! Her father will have you stoned! You can turn back now and run home. If you're quick, nobody will notice. Besides, what are you going to tell Him? Look at all those people! If you say you're unclean, they'll stone you before Yeshua can heal you!"

Erstis continued following the flow of the crowd, her feet stumbling along. A command from above had allowed Doubt to make one more attack on her. The two angels beside her held their swords pointed at Doubt. They allowed him one minute to tempt her, and then they pushed him away.

She could almost hear the clear voice of Faith speak to her. "You don't need to say anything to Him. He's Yahweh! He knows all about you, and about your sickness. He's expecting you. He wants to heal you! He loves you!"

Erstis sighed. Her mind raced to keep up with her thoughts, as things became clearer to her. *That's right. And He has the power to heal just by touching someone. So, all I have to do is touch Him, and I'll be healed! In fact, the tassels on the bottom of His prayer shawl represent the Torah, which is G-d's Word to us... and the Torah speaks of healing in the Word of Yahweh!* She was so thrilled that she felt as though she could burst.

If I can just touch the hem of His prayer shawl garment, I will be made whole! I won't even stop Him, or take any of His attention. Then He will continue on His way to heal the sick girl! We can both be healed and I won't be stoned!

She scurried down the street to her right.

I will get to the sandlemaker's before the crowd reaches there. Then, I will squeeze my way through the crowd to Yeshua and touch the hem of His prayer shawl, and then I will be healed. I will not give up on my life. I will be healed today!

She trudged on, not letting Fear or Doubt or Weakness stop her. Nor did she allow her pain or nausea to slow her down. She was on a mission to see Yeshua, and touch His robe. *Then, I will be made whole! I can hug and kiss my loved ones! I will be*

108

able to marry Moshe! Most importantly, I will be able to go to the
temple to hear the Torah again!

Finally, she could see the sandlemaker's house. To her dismay, the path was blocked with people, but because she was standing on a little knoll, she could see Yeshua with a group of men close about Him. Many men, women, and children were all jostling to get closer to Him.

She watched Yeshua for a moment. He looked around at the people pushing to be near Him. He glanced toward Erstis. Their eyes locked. He smiled. It lasted for only a second, but in that moment she felt more love and acceptance than she'd ever felt in her whole life.

"I must touch Yeshua!" she cried. "But how can I get through all these people?"

Strength whispered to her, "The Father will help you. Just take one step at a time."

109

CHAPTER SIX

Miracle of Miracles!

(Matthew 8:5-15, 23-27 & Mark 3:1-6; 5:29)

The closer she got to the crowd, the louder the river roared. The pushing and shoving of the crowd on this hot day was the complete opposite of the quiet, lonely days she'd endured for the past twelve years. Hundreds of heads — or possibly even a thousand — bobbed up and down in the stream of people.

Just as waves crash into one another, so people crashed into one another in the crowd. She waded into the stream, waves of dust lapping at her feet. The dry dust rose up and choked her as it caught in her throat. As one takes a deep breath and dives into the water, so Erstis took a deep breath and dove into the sea of people. She was determined.

*Now that I'm this close to Yeshua, I'm not going to turn back!*Erstis walked out a few feet, stepping sideways once in a while, as she worked her way closer to Yeshua in a zigzag fashion. All the noise, heat, and physical exertion made her dizzy and nauseated. She panted as she squirmed her way closer to the Messiah.

Suddenly, through the din of mingled voices, there came a clear voice that caught her attention. It was that of an older lady, but it was crisp and clear. "…the servant of the centurion in Capernaum. As soon as Yeshua entered the city the centurion came to Him and told Him that his servant was paralyzed and suffering dreadfully.

000   "Yeshua said He would go with the centurion to see the servant, but the man said he was unworthy to have Yeshua come to his home. He said that he was a man of authority and under authority. When he said to a soldier 'Go,' he would go; or when he said 'Come,' he would come. Then he said to Yeshua, 'Only speak a word and my servant will be healed.'"

Then Erstis heard another voice ask, "What did Yeshua do?"

The first voice responded, "He said He had not found such great faith in all of Israel. Then he said, 'go your way, what you have believed has been done.'"

"And…" prompted the second woman.

"And I've heard that his servant was healed that very same hour!"

Erstis took a deep breath and smiled. She plunged on ahead. *I know He's the Messiah! He doesn't even have to touch ᵗhe person. He just has to say the word and people are healed! I have to reach Him. If only I can touch him, I know that I will be healed!*

The Voice of Promise encouraged her to keep moving forward. "You have found favour in the eyes of the Lord. Because of your great faith, generation after generation will glorify the Lord G-d of Israel."

On she pushed, unaware of the angels around her, as well as of the demons flitting about overhead trying to get close enough to stab her with their swords. The demons were under strict orders: "Don't let her reach the Messiah!" They would stop at nothing to fulfill their mandate.

Erstis heard another clear voice through the buzz of the crowd. This one was that of a young woman. "I heard that he healed Peter's mother-in-law. She was lying sick with a fever. He touched her and the fever left. She even got up and served them dinner!"

Encouraged even more, Erstis squeezed between two men to get closer. She saw a head above the crowd. *That must be Him. I'm almost there!*

"Excuse me," she said again and again, as she pushed her way toward the front of the crowd. She was pushed this way then that way, and her feet were being stepped on. If she hadn't been so focused on reaching the Messiah, she would have taken a great deal of pleasure just to feel people touch her. It had been her great longing for the past twelve years.

As she broke through a group of men, she heard them speaking, "...were on a boat and a great tempest arose on the sea.

113

You heard about that huge storm that passed through here the other day. The waves were so high they covered the boat!"

"What did Yeshua do?" asked another.

"He was sleeping! His friends were afraid and they went to Him and woke Him up. They asked Him to save them. They said they were going to die!"

"Then what happened?"

"He asked them why they were so fearful and said they had such little faith."

"Then…"

"Then he got up. He rebuked the wind and the sea."

"What happened then?"

"What do you think? The sea became calm! The storm stopped!"

"Who is this man that even the winds and the sea obey Him?"

"Do you have to ask? Of course, He's the Messiah!"

Erstis took another deep breath and plunged on ahead of the group of men. Unknown to her, Hope was blowing the words toward her and cupped his hand around her ear to make her hear their words above all the loud noises that surrounded her.

Faith and Strength continued to do battle with Weakness and Doubt. The two stubborn demons continued swooping close toward Erstis, trying to stab at her with their swords. Putrid puffs streamed out of them where their scaly, black flesh was torn open by the angels' blazing swords. The angels were empowered to ward off the evil black creatures as long as she continued to call on the Father for strength.

Suddenly, Erstis stumbled over a rock on the path. She pitched forward onto a strong young man. "Hey!" he yelled as he jumped out of her way, "Watch where you're stepping, woman!"

Weakness had taken a jab at both Faith and Strength. That gave Doubt a chance to get to Erstis. He swooped down to her as the man shouted.

People around them turned to look as she struggled to stand to her feet. Doubt filled her mind. *People are noticing you! You're going to be stoned! You're unclean! You're not going to make it to Yeshua! You're going to die! Run home! Now! Run!*

Erstis took a deep breath as she noticed her veil was askew. She straightened it out and apologized to the man, "I am so sorry. Please, forgive me."

Did he see my skin?

Her heart pounded so loudly in her chest that she was sure everyone around her could hear it. *Surely this man saw me and would know that I am unclean. Maybe I will be stoned,* she thought as Doubt pierced her with his sword.

115

"Father Yahweh," she whispered, "Have mercy on me."

Just then, Hope swung his sword at Doubt, dislodging his sword and sending him sprawling in the dust. Hope leapt quickly onto him. He gave him a swift kick that sent him flying into the air.

Once again, Strength sliced into Weakness, and a fetid odour spewed from his wound. When he saw Doubt soar through the air, he slinked off to lick his wounds.

The man seemed to realize that the people around him might condemn him for his outburst to a woman, especially one in mourning. He reached out a strong arm to help her steady herself and said, "It is I who am sorry. I was impolite. Please, forgive me."

She nodded her head and said, "Thank you." The man turned to continue on his way.

Erstis breathed a huge sigh of relief. The crowd continued walking past her as she stood in shocked silence. *That was close!*

She sighed. She could still feel the pressure of his strong hand on her arm. *Oh, how wonderful it will be to feel Moshe's arms around me!*

Her body trembled. Whether it was from excitement or fear, she did not know. The danger had passed and people were pushing past her in droves. In a matter of seconds, she was much farther behind than she could imagine.

She took another deep breath and pushed her way forward. This time she headed toward the west side of the crowd. *Maybe I can move faster if I'm on the edge of the crowd.*

She was almost at the edge of the crowd when she heard more lucid voices. "…with a withered hand. Yeshua healed him on the Sabbath!"

"On the Sabbath? Is that lawful?"

"Lawful or not He did it! But first He asked the crowd, 'Is it lawful on the Sabbath to do good or to do evil, to save life or to kill?'"

"So He knew what people would think!"

"And He obviously thinks it is lawful."

Just then, Erstis broke free. She was now at the edge of the crowd. Quickly she surged forward. She couldn't see Yeshua's head anymore. *I must have fallen farther behind than I had thought. I'm going to make it!* She encouraged herself. *I know Yeshua is the Messiah and He will heal me! I have to get to Him!*

The crowd turned down a narrow street. Erstis found herself pinned between people and the buildings that lined the street. It seemed like the crowd was moving ahead without her. She was falling behind again.

117

From out of nowhere, Doubt came flying in and thrust his sword at Erstis, catching the angels unaware. *Will I ever get to Him? I keep falling behind!*

Faith was quick to knock a blow to the dark demon and send him and his sword flying away. Faith reassured Erstis, "Have faith! You will make it! Keep pressing on! You are going to be healed today! Today is your day! Keep going! You can do it!"

"I am going to be healed today!" Erstis said aloud. She caught her breath and looked around for fear that someone had heard her. Then she realized that there was so much noise and pushing and shoving that nobody could possibly have heard her.

Erstis took another deep breath of determination. She pushed forward saying, "Excuse me, please. Pardon me."

The crowd is squeezing closer and closer together. I can barely breathe! I must be getting close!

From off to the side, Weakness had slithered in along the ground. He struck his sword into Erstis' knees. All of a sudden, she felt as though her knees wanted to buckle beneath her weight.

She gasped for breath and reached out to steady herself, but there was nothing to hold onto, only the people who pushed up against her. Amazingly, however, that was enough to keep her upright.

Unseen to the throng, Strength gave Weakness a boot that sent him scuttling along the ground. Then Faith picked him up with one hand, and brought his other hand up in a fist to meet the slithering beast's stomach. Weakness groaned and doubled over in pain. Faith used both arms to pick him up high into the air. He threw him, sending him out of sight.

Erstis was determined. *Today, I'm going to see Yeshua. I'm going to be healed. Oh, how wonderful it will be to hug my sister and Mama, and Ruth, and Papa, and... Moshe!* At the thought of his name, she pushed forward with a greater urgency.

As she trudged on, she envisioned what Moshe had looked like twelve years ago. His bronze skin had glistened in the evening sun. She loved his gentle manner with children, but he was also strong. She remembered seeing him overpower a brawny bull. She surged ahead with determination that she would soon be wed.

All I have to do, her heart cried, *is get to Yeshua. I know that He'll heal me.* Suddenly, a force caught her from behind, dragging her beneath the surface. She landed face down, the dust flying up in her face. It made its way through her black veil, clogging her nostrils and filling her dry mouth. She gasped for breath.

Waves of people washed over her. She struggled to stay conscious. Breathing deeply, dust flew into her lungs. Every breath came out in a wheeze. As she got up on her hands and knees, someone slammed into her from the side. She sprawled out onto the dusty street again.

119

Dry sobs shook her body. When she opened her eyes, she saw hundreds of feet, some sandaled and some bare. A great thunder roared in her ears, as they all stormed past her.

With great resolve, she pushed herself up to her feet. *I'm going to touch Yeshua!* With her head down, she plunged forward. When she finally looked up, she saw Him. He was about six feet in front of her.

A sob caught in her throat. Even from behind, she felt the aura of love, and forgiveness about Him. His bearing spoke of authority, yet as He looked from side to side, His smile filled hearts with the love of Yahweh.

Now, it wasn't merely her determination pushing her forward, but also Yahweh's power and love drawing her to Yeshua — the Son of G-d!

At last, there was only one of His disciples — a big, burly man — between her and the Healer. *Now, I will just slip between those two men and touch Him.*

Just then, Faith swooped down and reminded her of the words of the prophet Malachi, "But unto you that fear my name shall the Sun of righteousness arise with healing in his wings."[12]

That's it! The tzitzit are the tassels that hang at the four corners of His prayer shawl! They're known as the "wings." There's healing in the tzitzit! If I can bend down, and touch the tassels of His prayer shawl, then I'll be healed! I can let the people will pass by me, and continue walking. Yeshua will go to heal the little girl, then, I will go and show myself to the priest.

She lifted her foot to step forward, but as she did, somebody rushed past her, which set her off balance. As she poised with one foot in the air, another person pushed by her. This sent her flying face first again. Her veil flew upwards, planting her face in the earth. Her mouth was filled with dry dirt.

She spit out the dirt. Shaking her head from side to side, she came back to her senses. She could barely see Yeshua's feet striding away as he headed off to see the dying girl.

*I **must** get to Him!*

She pushed herself to her hands and knees. She tossed the veil off her face so that it wouldn't get caught under her hands, and she squirmed between the feet of passers-by. She was mindless of the fact that the people could see her pale face.

As she crawled forward, sharp stones poked the skin on her hands and knees until they stung in pain.

Again she felt weak and dizzy. Squeezing her eyes shut for a moment, she fought against the nausea. She continued crawling like a baby. The dust flew in her face, making her breathing laboured. People kicked her as they walked by.

Excruciating pain seared through her fingers, up to her elbow. She gasped as a large man lifted his dusty foot off of her bony hand. The heat, normally causing sweat to pour, caused her

121

dried skin to crack. She knew from the intense pain in her abdomen that blood was flowing profusely.

Suddenly, Pride, a large demon that hadn't bothered Erstis in years, dove through the crowd and stabbed the crawling figure with discouraging thoughts.

"You proud woman!" he said, "Don't you know that if you make it to Yeshua, He'll condemn you for being so proud of yourself? Look at you trying so hard time and again! You think you can do it all on your own strength! You're an evil woman! You don't deserve to be healed. You will be humiliated in front of everyone for your pride. Then you'll be stoned for breaking the law! You're going to die!"

Of the three angels that had been walking with her, Peace now circled above the throng of people. They all saw Pride attack her, and allowed him the few seconds allotted to him. It may have only been seconds, but to Erstis, it felt interminable. She quickly cried out, "Abba, Father, please help me!"

Peace spiralled down through the crowd, and took a swipe at Pride. Reluctantly, Pride released his hold on Erstis. He and Peace swooped high into the sky, swords gleaming and clashing in the bright sun.

Suddenly, from the side, someone kicked Erstis, sending her sprawling in the dirt again. "Father Yahweh!" she cried as she struggled to get up again. "Forgive me for my sin. I know that there is nothing that I can do to heal myself. It is only Your great mercy upon this sinner that can cleanse me. I know that Yeshua is the Messiah. He is Your Son, oh Lord. Please give me strength to reach Him!"

At her plea for strength, the broad-shouldered angel swooped down and picked her up, standing her upright on her feet. She pulled the veil back down over her dirt-streaked face, before standing on the tips of her toes to see Yeshua. *Oh, He's so far away again...*

On she marched. Faith walked in front of Erstis, opening a path for her. Strength walked beside her, ministering to her weak body with strength. She was finally getting closer to Yeshua when the angels reluctantly backed off, and let her go on alone. They resumed their protection from above the thronging crowd.

As people pushed and shoved all around Erstis, she felt peculiarly light and agile, even though she was still hot and dirty. The pain numbed, and her nauseous tummy stopped rolling. The world about her came into focus for a moment, and she sighed. *I must be a sight!*

Once again, she found herself directly behind the burly disciple. She heard someone call him Simon Peter. He smelled of fish — an odour she hadn't smelled for years. It sent her stomach reeling again. The world began to spin like a top.

Another man was leading Yeshua right nearby. Erstis was sure that he was the little girl's father.

I'm this close! I can't fail now!

In a burst of reckless abandon, she threw herself forward, reaching out to touch the tassels of the Messiah's prayer shawl.

She landed on the ground with a thud. The impact caused her to gasp for breath. *I must stay conscious,* she commanded herself, fighting to retain a grasp on reality. *He's getting away!*

She felt people stepping over her and walking around her. With a grunt and a groan, she heaved herself up on all fours again. Throwing back the veil, she put her head down, like a bull about to charge. She pushed forward, weaving in and out between pairs of legs.

She was oblivious to the dust in her face, and the stones cutting into her hands and knees. What did it matter? She was on her way to Yeshua.

Finally, she crawled up behind Simon Peter. She could feel the love of Yahweh permeating from Yeshua. Filled with excitement that her dream was finally about to be fulfilled, she began sobbing softly, but as was usual for her, no tears flowed. Her parched throat throbbed from the dry sobs, and from the heat and the dust.

Being filled with humility and awe in the presence of Yahweh, Erstis squeezed between the two disciples. There, right in front of her, were the feet of Yeshua!

Reaching out her hand she touched the tassels that dangled in front of her. She was filled with a holy awe, as she realized that she was touching the Word of Yahweh in the flesh, not just a representation in cloth.

As her fingers connected with the soft tassels, an overwhelming power surged through her fingertips, up into her arm, and throughout her entire body.

Crouched on her knees, she brought her hand up to her face, oblivious of the people passing by all around her. As the sensation spread down her other arm, she held it out, staring at it, as if she could see something different about it.

The wonderful sensation went up into her head, dispelling her dizziness. Suddenly, the world came sharply into focus. The spinning stopped. Houses and trees in the distance that were once fuzzy shapes now had distinct features.

Although the whole process took only a matter of seconds, it seemed to Erstis that time stood still. She felt the power go into her chest. She inhaled deeply through her nose, and the scents of fish, flowers, and fresh bread filled her being. As that happened, the powerful sensation continued on down into her ribs and abdomen. Amazingly, the nausea ceased even while Erstis was inhaling the many conflicting odours that were swirling about her in the air.

Suddenly the pain, along with the feeling of the blood flowing in her abdomen, came to a halt. Overwhelmed by the reality, and by the mercy and grace of Yahweh, Erstis began to weep. To her amazement, she no longer had the dry hacking sobs that had caused her throat to ache.

125

Salty teardrops squeezed their way out of her tear ducts, tracing a path down her sallow cheeks and dripping off the tip of her chin. Saliva ran down the back of her throat. She blinked her eyes, and then swallowed, as if unfamiliar with the fluid her body was suddenly producing.

I'm healed! she realized.

She wanted to run up and down the street shouting, "I'm whole!" But resting her face in her hands, she continued to weep, praising Yahweh for healing her. She lifted up her hands in praise to Yeshua, the Messiah!

Suddenly, she was startled by a rumbling in her stomach! With wonder and joy, she realized that she was hungry, for the first time in years.

She laughed aloud, and threw back her black veil and shedding the gloves. *I have to go tell Mama!*

Just as she was about to get up, she noticed that the rushing river of people had become a placid lake. She looked about her. Everything was still and quiet. No one dared to breathe.

She gasped when she heard Yeshua speak.

"Who touched Me?"

CHAPTER SEVEN

The Thief Comes to Steal and Destroy!

The angels rejoiced and glorified the Master. Erstis had been healed. The celebration only lasted for a few seconds, however. The angels sobered as they realized that Erstis was about to encounter the most difficult test of all — and once again, the angels had to let her face the test alone. They could protect her physical body, but her mind would be tempted. A bright light, not noticeable by humans, shone above the crowd as the angels soared above, keeping an ever-watchful eye over Erstis.

The hulking form of Fear hovered over Erstis. He thrust his sharp talons into her head. Then it occurred to her: *He knows that I touched Him!*

Simon Peter asked Yeshua, "Master, what do You mean by asking 'Who touched me?'" He gestured toward the crowd. "The people are thronging about. Hundreds are pushing and shoving to get near You, and yet You ask, 'Who touched Me?'" Peter threw his arms in the air and shook his head from side to side.

Erstis' eyes bulged as she realized that her actions were about to be revealed to the crowd. What would happen? Fear sunk his talons deeper into her skull. "He'll condemn you. It won't last.

You're going to start bleeding again! Then they will stone you for being in public when you're unclean. You've put all of their lives in danger. You will pay for this with your life! You're going to die! They're going to kill you!"

She began to tremble. *I **know** that the power of G-d flowed through my body!*

As soon as that thought entered her mind, Fear tightened his grip onto her emotions. "You'd better run home and hide before anyone realizes what a dreadful sin you've committed. Run quickly! Run! Run!"

Erstis shook her head from side to side. Amazingly, she didn't feel dizzy at all. She leaped to her feet with determined resolve. Still no dizzy sensation. *I **am** healed! Yeshua **is** the Messiah!*

She began to approach Yeshua. The angels swooped down and made a way for her to go forward. Strength gently guided her toward the Master.

Fear had lost his grip on her. Now he battled with Peace. As swords clanged, he swooped down and tried to fill her mind with fear again. "Don't go! They'll stone you! Run home! Don't tell anyone! You need to hide! Run!"

Erstis ignored the fearful thoughts. As she walked closer to Yeshua, and inevitably closer to what could have been her impending death, she heard Yeshua speak.

His voice rang out clearly across the crowd. Now Erstis understood how the large crowds of people could hear Him so well. His voice held authority, like Aunt Rachel had told her; it was as if He owned the world. Yet His voice was also filled with compassion, as if He genuinely cared about the one who had touched Him.

"I felt power go out from me," He said.

So, He felt it too! She watched Him scan the crowd. When His dark brown eyes came to rest on her, He held her gaze. He knew that she was the one who had touched Him. To Erstis, it was like looking into a pool of compassion. A sense of peace emanated from Him. She felt loved and accepted, and she stood still, gazing into His eyes.

People began to follow His eyes to see who He was looking at. As they realized Yeshua was looking at Erstis, however, they began to back away. Like the Red Sea, the human river parted and Erstis ran toward Yeshua. She dropped to her knees at His feet.

Salty tears rolled down her cheeks as she cried out, "Master, I've been unclean…"

As she spoke, she heard cries far off in the crowd. Erstis recognized the voices of her sister and her cousin.

"What has she done?" cried Hannah. Arm in arm, tears streaming down their cheeks, Hannah and Ruth made their way toward Erstis and Yeshua. "She's already on the verge of death. Surely she will be stoned!"

When the crowd realized that the small woman that had been among them was unclean, they gasped in unison and backed away even further. People began to murmur and grumble. The word "stoned" bobbed up and down on the angry waves of the human river.

As much as they didn't want to see it happen, Hannah and Ruth would not leave Erstis alone at such a time. They pressed forward, determined to protect her at any cost.

By the time Erstis finished telling her story to Yeshua, Hannah and Ruth had broken through the ring of people that encircled the two. The young lady kneeling before the Messiah had finished speaking. A great hush enveloped the crowd.

Yeshua gazed lovingly at the weeping girl. Feeling His gaze steadily on her, she reluctantly looked up and met His eyes. There she saw understanding and forgiveness. It seemed that He knew all that she had been through, as if He had been with her through the last twelve difficult years. He shared her loneliness and isolation. His gaze was overflowing with love and acceptance. It wrapped itself around Erstis like a warm cloak.

Finally, He spoke. The words were directed at her, but they were clear and loud enough for all to hear, "Daughter, your faith has made you well. Go in peace, and be healed of your affliction."

A gasp rose from the crowd. Whispers were passed around as they realized that the young woman in black was Erstis — the poor girl with the issue of blood. Doctors had given up on her, but Yeshua had healed her! He had just proclaimed healing and peace to the young woman! The air was filled with excitement. Nobody would be willing to throw the first stone now. Erstis was free from the bondage of sickness, and free from the penalty of the law. She was indeed a free woman now!

"I'm healed!" cried Erstis. "Yeshua has healed me and set me free!"

With a shout, Hannah and Ruth ran to Erstis, their arms outstretched. Erstis heard their cry and turned to them. Her arms were open wide and tears still streamed down her face.

When the two young women saw that Erstis shed tears, they realized that she had indeed been healed. The three women hugged one another, all talking at once as Yeshua looked upon them and smiled.

Erstis closed her eyes as she squeezed her cousin and her sister tightly. Their skin was soft. Emotion bubbled up within her. The fountain of tears that had been dried up for years now burst forth in a gush. *For so long I've dreamed of this day. Yet, it is even better than I've ever dreamed!* Tingles went through her hands as she caressed her loved ones.

From behind Him, Yeshua seemed to sense — rather than hear — that the Rulers of the Synagogue had come with bad news. Jarius, who had been at Yeshua's side, moved his weight

133

from one foot to the other. "Master, we must hurry to my daughter," he pleaded. They both turned to see the bearer of bad news arrive.

The spokesman said to Jarius, "Come now, my friend. Your daughter has already died. There is no need to bother the Master anymore. There is nothing more to do, but to come and join your wife. She has already begun to mourn."

Jarius cried out in anguish as he buried his face in his hands. "No!" he wailed as he tore at his clothes. The news-bearer put his arms around Jarius, and guided him toward his home.

Yeshua reached out and rested his hand on Jarius' shoulder. The man lifted his eyes of sorrow to look into pools of love and sympathy in Yeshua's eyes.

Yeshua spoke softly, "Take me to her." It was not a question. It was a demand, lathered in compassion and authority. "I want only Peter, James, and John to follow me." The men turned to go.

The three women, who had been huddled together, pulled apart to listen to the sad announcement. Before the news-bearer had finished speaking, the hulking form of Guilt descended on Erstis like a vulture upon his prey.

He dove down with his claws ready to puncture his victim. His talons pierced her head, filling her thoughts. *It is all my fault! If I hadn't stopped Yeshua for my own needs, He could have healed her before it was too late. I am selfish! I don't deserve the healing I received. In fact, the healing I received was meant for that sick little girl. I stole her healing from her! I'm a horrible person!*

Erstis hadn't been paying attention to Ruth and Hannah. She had been consumed with guilt. Suddenly, Hannah's voice penetrated the demonic thoughts. "Erstis! What's the matter?"

"Oh," she gasped as she became aware of her sister's voice, "I was just feeling bad for that poor little girl. Maybe if I hadn't bothered Yeshua He would have gotten to her in time to heal her."

"Sweetie..." Hannah put a smoothing arm around Erstis' thin shoulders. "Don't feel that way. Just be grateful that you are whole again. Remember in the Torah, the prophet Jeremiah said, 'For I will forgive their iniquity, and I will remember their sin no more.'[13] Let's go show you to the priest, and make the required sacrifice. Then, we'll go see Mama and Papa. I'm so sorry that I didn't have faith to bring you myself. You have such strong faith…" She babbled on, thrilled about her sister's healing and great faith.

Meanwhile, a bright light flashed out from a big tree, right toward Erstis. The Grateful spirit came up behind Guilt and charged him, causing him to release his hold on Erstis. The impact vaulted him through the air, depositing him in a crumpled pile in a tree a hundred feet away.

The human eye could see the leaves and branches move ever so slightly, as if the wind was blowing. In reality, the weight of Guilt caused the branches to spread, and let Guilt fall to the ground. In a silent swoop, Gratefulness flew over to finish him off.

Erstis smiled at her sister. "Thank you! You're right. How can I be sad on such a blessed day?" She linked arms with Ruth and Hannah, squeezing them tightly. The three women skipped toward the temple.

When they reached the fork in the road, Erstis stopped in her tracks. To veer left would take them to the temple, but to go right would take them home. Her sister and cousin looked at her, silently asking her why she had stopped.

Erstis looked toward her Mama's house. With a deep yearning she said, "I want to see Mama and Papa so much! Let us go home first. Then I can wash and change my clothes before I go to the priest."

"That's a wonderful idea, Erstis," Ruth responded as she squeezed the arm of her dear friend and cousin. Erstis knew Ruth was relishing the fact that now she could touch her once more. Although she could feel her bones through the thin layer of skin, it wouldn't be long until she would gain some weight. She reminded herself, *Now that I am healed, I will be able to eat again.*

"However," Ruth continued with a mischievous gleam in her eyes, "I have a better idea. Come to my house, and wash. Then you can don one of my gowns. I have a beautiful tan gown that Joseph bought me, but until I have delivered this child I

136

won't fit into it. I know it will look lovely on you. After that, we'll come with you to see your Mama and Papa."

Erstis thought about it for a moment. A smile broke across her face, like the sun breaking through the clouds. "As much as I'm anxious to see them, I would like to clean up and put on something new and clean for them to see me in. Let's do it!"

The three of them walked arm in arm to Ruth's house. As they drew close to the house Aunt Rachel came out the front door. "Who on earth can that be?" she asked herself aloud. "It looks like Erstis! But it can't be. She's unclean!"

When Erstis saw her, she couldn't hold back any longer. She sprinted to her aunt. Arms open wide, she shouted, "It's me, Aunt Rachel! Yeshua the Messiah has healed me! I am whole again!"

Aunt Rachel slowly drew closer to Erstis. She squinted her eyes as she peered at Erstis running toward her like a young girl. With outstretched arms and tears streaming down her face, Rachel cried, "Erstis! You're running! And you're crying real tears! Surely Jehovah has made you whole!"

By the time they reached each other, Aunt Rachel knew for sure that Yeshua had indeed made her well again.

"Oh, you blessed child!" she crooned as she held her weeping niece. Then she pulled her away. "Let me look at you! You're crying! And you were running! Do you not feel weak?"

137

"I feel wonderful!" exalted Erstis. "The pain is gone! So is the nausea and dizziness. I'm completely whole! My body, which has not produced a tear in years, is somehow overflowing with tears! Glory to G-d in the highest!"

By this time, Ruth and Hannah had joined them. "You did take a terrible risk," reprimanded Aunt Rachel. "Don't you know that you could have gotten yourself stoned, going out in public like that?"

"But dear Aunt Rachel, can't you try to understand? Yahweh knows everything. This Yeshua is the Messiah — Yahweh's Son! He knew that I needed to be healed. He *wanted* to heal me. He wouldn't let me be stoned. Don't you see?"

"Well," sniffed the concerned Aunt, "how do you know that they won't stone you once the word gets around the town?"

"Mama," responded Ruth as she put a restricting hand on her Mama's arm, "let us be joyful, and praise Yahweh for the miracle He has done. And we will *all* have faith that Yahweh will protect her in the future. Besides, Yeshua told her to 'Go in peace.' Nobody will harm her. She's clean now!"

As she spoke, Ruth linked arms with Erstis and her Mama. Hannah hooked arms on the other side of her sister. Together, they walked toward the house while Ruth explained the plan to her Mama.

******

As Erstis lathered the soap, she scrubbed every bit of uncleanness away. She dreamed of being together with her Mama and Papa, and with all of her friends and relatives. *It has been so long since I've seen my little brothers…*

Suddenly, she felt Fear enter the room, and her thoughts changed. *What if you start to bleed again? What if your Papa won't have you back? What about Moshe? He probably won't ever have you. You'll still never be able to bear children. He'll reject you for that!*

Unbidden tears of sadness welled up in her eyes. Up until that point, all her tears had been tears of joy and repentance.

She prayed silently. *Lord, I know that You healed me, and You love me. I will trust You to keep my future.*

Then she said aloud, "I know whom I have believed, and I am convinced that He is able to keep what I have committed to Him against that day."[14]

She dried herself as she declared, "I will go to Mama and Papa, and I *will* live my long life for Yahweh!"

CHAPTER EIGHT

Confession

Hanging high in the sky, the sun burned across the parched land. Aunt Rachel had gone for a visit with her sister, Mary. The plan was for Rachel to get to Erstis' mother's house before any nosey gossips arrived. People loved to be the first one to tell a tale. Erstis wanted to be the one to tell her Mama of her expedition earlier that day, and of the amazing news of Yeshua healing her.

Hannah and Ruth helped Erstis dress in one of Ruth's best dresses. The long tan gown accented her pale skin, but Erstis noticed that her skin already had more colour to it. She was still very pale for a Jew, but she knew it would not be long until her olive skin would declare her Jewish heritage once again.

Erstis fingered the light material. For twelve long years she had only worn rough rags. The silky, soft gown slipped on her smooth skin. Hannah and Ruth stood back to take in the effect. Ruth had washed Erstis' long, scraggly hair, and trimmed the uneven ends. Her cheeks now glowed with excitement.

The effect caused Hannah to choke back a sob. "Bless Yahweh! I thought I never would see this day!" Ruth put a consoling arm around her cousin, and she started to sing softly…

"Great is the Lord, and greatly to be praised

In the city of our G-d

In His holy mountain

Beautiful in elevation

The joy of the whole earth,

Is Mount Zion on the sides of the north,

The city of the great King."[15]

Erstis and Hannah joined in the singing, and Erstis even began to spin about the small house as she sang. She flung her arms in the air and danced like a butterfly fluttering in the wind. She flitted about and twirled like a young girl.

Hannah caught her arm and said, "Erstis, honey, take it easy. You don't want to wear yourself out before you see Mama and Papa!"

"And the priest!" she gasped, coming to an abrupt halt.

"But Erstis," declared Hannah, "I just realized! You can't go to the priest until seven days have passed!"

"Oh, that's right," realized Erstis. "In all the excitement, I forgot about that!"

142

"So did I," admitted Ruth.

Suddenly, out of the silence came a rumbling gurgling sound from Erstis' stomach. Hannah and Ruth's eyes bulged, and Erstis giggled as she clutched her tummy. "I'm hungry," she confessed.

The other two girls joined in the giggling. "Come on, let me get you a bit of bread," said Ruth, leading the way.

As they walked, Erstis chattered on, "This is the first time in years that I've felt hungry. It is so strange. Glory to Yahweh! And I don't feel nauseated any more, either."

She sunk her teeth into a chewy morsel of bread. As she chewed, she savoured the sweet flavor. "Mmmm... This is *delicious*!" As she swallowed bite after bite, she felt the food fill her tummy.

Bread means "life". How significant it is that the first thing I eat after being healed is bread — life! She wondered how the Gentiles could cut bread with a knife. Didn't they know it represented stabbing and cutting life?

Ruth brought her a cup of tea. She slowly sipped the hot drink. "Oh," she crooned, "this is *so* much better than that terrible milk! Ugh! I never want to drink milk ever again!"

"And you will *never* have to drink that stuff ever again!" empathized Ruth as she linked arms with her cousin, and led her toward the door. "Now, let's go see your Mama!"

143

Hannah and Eristis walked, skipped, and ran in turn toward their parents' home. Ruth, feeling quite heavy in her pregnancy, kept a steady walking pace. As they walked through the streets, the neighbours and townsfolk noticed the three young women strolling merrily along. They could not recognize Erstis as the woman who had been cursed by the issue of blood when she was only a girl. They could, however, deduce who she was by the fact that she was with her sister and cousin.

Rumours of Erstis' healing flew across the town like a swarm of bees after a honey thief. As they walked past the potter's house, his son realized who she was. He tugged at his Mama's arm, "Mama, look! Isn't that the woman that Yeshua healed this morning?"

The mother gasped, bringing her hand up to her throat, "You're right! It is her!"

The boy shouted, "Come on, Isaiah! Let's go see her!" As he took off running toward Erstis, his twin brother ran to catch up to him. The woman, gathering her younger offspring, set off to collect the two boys before they caused a scene.

Before she could catch up with the mischievous twins, other people had noticed and joined them, too. Soon, a large crowd had gathered behind the three happy women. The group stayed behind them, wanting to get close, but feeling hesitant. Some still feared that she could be slightly unclean, yet others wanted to hear every bit of conversation that was floating on the air around them.

The three young ladies led the crowd through the town to Erstis' parents' house. Erstis felt wonderful now that she could skip ahead and twirl in circles, with her arms fluttering in the air. Carefree, she sang praises to Yahweh.

The Father had given the command — the demons could not touch her now. There would be no more tests. She had passed each one with faith and courage. Now a great host of mighty angelic warriors enveloped her. Demons would not be sneaking in to harass her any longer.

The crowd behind her grew larger and larger. By the time they reached their destination, the crowd had become a huge mob, thronging to get a better view of the dying daughter's reunion with her grieving Mama.

*****

Unknown to Mary, while she was having tea with her sister Rachel, the crowd was on its way to her door. The two women, only two years apart in age, had always been close. Many times they would even think the same thoughts, and then speak identical sentences at the same time.

The two sisters still giggled like they did when they were children, and oftentimes tears of joy would stream down their faces. Unlike the other men of their day, their husbands never

145

complained about the frequent visits between the two women. They both agreed that their wives were younger, happier, and healthier because of their love for each other.

On this warm, dry day, Mary noticed that Rachel had been acting very strangely. There was nothing abnormal about the fact that she had come over for tea, of course — she often did so. The strange thing was that she arrived with a glow on her face, yet she denied the fact that she knew of anything special that might have caused it. Normally, the two women talked continuously. Today, however, the conversation seemed to lag. Rachel often appeared to be lost in thought.

"Rachel?" Mary nudged her sister.

"Oh, I'm sorry. What did you say?"

"How is Ruth feeling?" Mary repeated her question.

"She says she feels as big as an ox. But she's doing well, bless Yahweh!"

"Her time must be very near."

No response.

"Rachel?" prodded Mary.

"Hmm? Oh… yes."

Finally, Mary sat back and sighed. She wondered what was going on. Mary knew, however, that her sister would share it

146

with her when she was ready. The sister watched silently as Rachel stood up and wandered to the stove to stoke the fire.

Rachel picked up the teapot and asked, "Mary, why don't you have another cup of tea?" Although it was Mary's home, Rachel felt comfortable offering her sister tea in her own home.

As Mary turned to look at Rachel, she noticed that her sister, who had been peering intently out of the window, jerked her head away from the window to face her. Mary wondered what Rachel was looking for.

"Thank you, honey," replied Mary, "I'd love another cup of tea."

As Rachel poured the tea, she started muttering something about a new tea that Joseph had bought for Ruth from a travelling merchant. While she spoke, she wandered back over to the window, appearing to glance casually outside. A cloud of dust was rising on this side of the potter's house. Rachel's breath caught in her throat as she realized that the girls must be on their way. Judging by the size of the dust cloud that followed, she could tell that a large crowd was coming with them, too. She knew that the curiosity of people would be roused by the girls' short journey.

Mary had been watching her sister closely. She wondered again why Rachel kept looking out her window. Was she afraid of something? No. After a closer look at Rachel's face, Mary realized that she actually seemed very excited about something that was happening outside.

147

Finally, Mary could not stand it any longer. She stood to her feet, her cup still in her hand, and strode toward the door. "Rachel, since you're so fond of looking outside, why don't we just take our tea out front and visit there?"

Rachel's last glance told her that they had almost arrived. "Oh, there's no need to do that," she said as she grasped Mary's hand. Using a little more force than necessary, she pried Mary's hand from the door. Guiding her back to her seat, she said, "Just sit down and drink your tea while I tell you about Jarius' daughter. Have you heard what happened to her?"

Mary allowed herself to be redirected back to her seat, knowing that if her sister wanted to surprise her with something, it wouldn't be very loving to spoil the surprise. Aloud, she asked, "Jarius… he's the Ruler of the Synagogue?"

"That's right," Rachel joined Mary, and told her the story of Jarius and Yeshua — omitting the part about Erstis, of course.

*****

As the mob rounded the bend, the farm came into view. The little house stood nestled between two sycamore trees. The stream in the west field rushed down from the mountains. The cold water gurgled and splashed its way through the farm, irrigating the fields around it.

148

Birds chirped and twittered about. It was as if they knew about Erstis' experience and were declaring the glory of Yahweh to all who were near. Butterflies fluttered lightly all around. The braying of the donkey could be heard from the barn. The smell of manure mixed with dirt wafted through the air.

Suddenly, Erstis' emotions welled up within her. Like a water fountain, tears burst forth at the sight of the farm she had grown up on. It was like the dead were coming to life. The farm had been dead to Erstis. She had thought she would never set foot on it again. Now, here she was — alive and well, and walking onto the farm.

Erstis slowly came to a halt. Ruth and Hannah put their arms about her in empathy and encouragement. The crowd gathered around, shuffling into position to get the best possible view of what would happen next.

*****

Inside the house, Rachel had just finished telling Mary about the death of Jarius' daughter, when she sensed that the mob had entered the yard.

Now that she knew Erstis had arrived, her eyes lit up, and she told her sister about a woman who had crawled through the

149

dust and dirt amongst the crowd to touch the tzitzit of Yeshua's prayer shawl — and was healed!

As she related the tale to Mary, she stood up once more and walked to the window. What she saw confirmed what she had already sensed. Her eyes widened as she saw the magnitude of the crowd.

As if on cue, Mary asked, "What was she healed of?"

Rachel smiled radiantly as tears pooled in her eyes. She replied, "She had an issue of blood."

She continued talking as she walked over to Mary, prompted her to get up, and walk to the door. "The woman had been suffering for twelve long years and the doctors had given up hope of her ever getting well. She was dying."

As Rachel opened the door, she gently prodded Mary to go out ahead of her. She couldn't see Mary's brows furrow. To Mary, Rachel's story made it sound like the woman had been suffering just like Erstis — but she didn't know of anyone else in the village that suffered with the same affliction for the same number of years.

With a dramatic flourish of her hand, Rachel announced, "The young woman that Yeshua healed was none other than our very own…" Mary walked out into the sunlight, to face the huge crowd. She frowned in confusion.

She noticed three girls standing front and centre, surrounded by the huge crowd. Mary immediately recognized Hannah and Ruth, who had accompanied a third young lady. Struggling to comprehend the significance of the situation, she noticed that the girl in the very centre wore a beautiful tan dress. Her long black hair shone in the afternoon sun. The matching veil covered the top part of her head.

As Mary looked at the face of the slender young girl, she saw that it was Erstis. Confusion filled her mind, for she knew it was unlawful for Erstis to touch anyone. How could she be standing in the midst of this large crowd? Realization dawned on her, at the same time as Rachel completed her long drawn out sentence. "…Erstis! She was made whole! Yeshua has healed your daughter!"

Mary gasped. Tears immediately sprang into her eyes as the magnitude of the situation filled her mind. Her heart leaped into her throat, causing her to swallow again in an effort to remove the lump in her throat. "My baby! She's well again!" she cried. "Glory to Yahweh!" With a stream of tears flowing down her face, she ran toward her daughter, arms outstretched.

Erstis sprinted toward her Mama. Shocked to see her daughter running, Mary slowed down to a stumbling walk. "You're running! And weeping?" she uttered as her hands came up to cover her mouth. She stumbled, as if in slow motion, toward her daughter.

Erstis called out, "Mama! Yeshua has healed me! I can run again!"

151

Mary threw open her arms again, and finally engulfed her daughter in a long-awaited hug. The river of tears that flowed from Mary mingled with those bursting forth from Erstis, causing both women to taste the salty tears as they laughed and cried together.

Shivers tingled down Erstis' spine as she felt her Mama's strong arms around her. *Oh, how nice she smells! Thank you, Yahweh, for healing me and allowing me to touch and hold my dear Mama again! Bless Your Holy Name!* Her Mama's touch permeated warmth, love, and strength.

How wonderful to feel the embrace of my sweet Mama. Yahweh, words can't express my gratefulness to You.

Many onlookers in the crowd shed tears that day. The words of Yeshua had turned their hostile hearts toward peace.

"Yeshua healed me, Mama!" breathed Erstis again, as she squeezed her Mama tightly. She pulled away to look at her. "He made me whole. I'm not unclean anymore! Yeshua *is* the Messiah, Mama! I know by the power that flowed into my body when I touched Him — and by the way He looked at me! Oh, Mama! Words cannot describe the look — it was loving… forgiving…" At a loss for words, she trailed off.

"I know, dear. I have seen Him. There are no words that can do Him justice. He is indeed sent from G-d." She put her arm around Erstis' waist and told Ruth, Rachel and Hannah,

"Please, let us go indoors, out of the sun, and rest while

we hear the story from Erstis." As they turned to walk into the house, the crowd slowly began to disperse.

Once they were inside, Aunt Rachel went about preparing cool, refreshing drinks while Erstis sat down with her mother and sister on either side of her. "Where's Papa?" Ersits asked, as she began to look around the house, remembering the place where she had grown up. *I lived here twelve whole years ago…*

"Your Papa has gone out of town with Benjamin. He's looking into some new grain seeds."

"Benjamin..." Erstis let her younger brother's name roll off her tongue. "He was only six when I became ill. And he's married now."

"Yes, he is."

"But when is Papa going to return?" interrupted Erstis, in her eagerness to see her Papa.

"Oh, he'll be back for dinner tomorrow."

"Not until tomorrow? How can I wait?" cried Erstis.

"Well," her Mama mused softly, "it has been twelve long years. How much longer can one day seem?"

"Oh, Mama, I know. I'm just so excited and—" Her tummy rumbled. She covered her mouth with her hand as she giggled, "I'm hungry again."

"Hungry?" queried her Mama and Aunt Rachel in unison.

"You just ate!" declared Hannah.

Aunt Rachel was already moving about the house, finding some bread and slicing some cheese for Erstis.

Ruth gave Erstis a pat on the arm. "Well, I have no doubt that we'll get some flesh back on your bones in no time!"

Laughter filled the house and trickled out to the few onlookers that remained by the roadside.

"And where is Little Luke?" asked Erstis.

Again the room erupted in laughter. "You still call him 'Little Luke' do you?" queried cousin Ruth. "When you see him, you won't say the word 'little' in his presence again!"

"A hulk of a man!" stated Aunt Rachel.

"He's taken the herd to graze in the hills. He's expected to be gone a fortnight.[16]" At Erstis' crest fallen look, she hastened to add, "He's been gone seven days already."

"Well, I see that my family still stays quite busy." Erstis sighed, and then grew quiet.

The room grew very still. Finally, her Mama asked, "What is it, honey? What has your thoughts occupied on such a joyous day?"

"Oh, it's just that I was thinking about..." she spoke so quietly that her words trailed off before she even finished her sentence. She stared out the window, lost in a dream of long ago.

Ruth put her hand on Erstis' arm again. Softly she whispered, "Moshe?" It was more of a statement than a question — a completion of the unfinished sentence.

Erstis pulled her mind out of her reverie and turned back to her family. She smiled, "Yes, Moshe. I wondered where he is and what he's doing now..." Once again she trailed off, as if not really expecting an answer.

"Well..." began Hannah, "remember I said that I saw him the other day?" Erstis jerked her head up as she came to attention.

"Certainly I do! Go on, please!" she urged.

"I didn't want to tell you all of it, lest your hopes be shattered. He has a farm of his own now, in the south part of town. He has been raising sheep, and is quite prosperous. He mentioned that he was taking his herd up into the hills for grazing. I think he said he would be back the day after Sabbath."

"Four days," moaned Erstis. "How shall I endure the wait?"

"That's easy!" cried Hannah, "Cousin Ruth is going to have a baby soon. We need to prepare for that. We also need to prepare a new wardrobe for you and make plans for the future.

155

We don't need the men for that. We'll have a great time without them!"

The five continued their visit, planning to have a grand party once "Little Luke" returned in seven days' time. After twelve years of being cut off from the world around her, Erstis was going to be the centre of the celebration. Later that night, they went to Aunt Rachel's home for dinner.

On the way, the women stopped at the Synagogue so that Erstis could show herself to the priest. Under normal conditions, she would have waited seven days. However, the Messiah had come and He had healed her. Just like the many lepers that had been healed by Yeshua, Erstis showed the priest that Yeshua had made her completely well.

It was quite clear to everyone that she truly was healed. All vomiting, dizziness, and pain were gone. In their place were hunger and strength. Aunt Rachel fried a succulent fish for dinner that night, and Erstis savoured every bite.

The next morning dawned bright and clear. Mary wakened to the melodic voice of her eldest daughter. Erstis had risen with the sun, like she often dreamed of doing again. She merrily puttered about the kitchen, making a delicious breakfast. The glories of Yahweh poured out from her heart in song.

Mother and daughter enjoyed a wonderful day together. As the sun headed for the western sky, the two women began to prepare a beautiful meal for Papa and Benjamin's return. The meal was in its final stages when Erstis heard the sound of

156

donkeys coming into the yard. She jumped up with a squeal, "Papa's coming!"

In a flash she burst out the front door and down the pathway toward her father. As she went she shouted, "Papa! Yeshua made me whole! I'm healed! I'm clean again!"

As her father walked into the yard he looked up to see a wonderful sight — his daughter, Erstis, running down the lane toward him with her arms wide open. As her words reached him, an overwhelming gratitude filled his heart. Yahweh had healed his baby girl! She would not die anytime soon! "Praise and glory be to G-d!" he shouted as he ran toward Erstis with his arms outstretched.

As they came together, the father engulfed his daughter in a tight embrace.

Erstis squeezed her papa tightly. *Oh, how I have missed this feeling.*

"How did this happen? Tell me all about it! Let me look at you!" The father pulled away to look at his beautiful daughter.

Already the colour had come back to Erstis' skin. She knew he could see a difference. Her hair shone in the sunlight and her face glowed. "Amazing!" he said.

Together the two walked back to the house, arm-in-arm. Erstis began to tell her father the story of what had transpired over

157

the last week. She leaned her head against her father. *How good it feels to be in his strong arms again!*

Just as the two reached the house, they heard a noise coming from the road. They turned to see who was coming their way. What Erstis saw filled her heart with delight. A young man, bronze-skinned with compassionate brown eyes, tall of stature and well built. He had been riding a donkey, but he leaped off the beast and ran toward Erstis and her father. He shouted, "Erstis! Is it true? Have you been healed?"

Erstis' face lit up like the sun. She gave her Papa's hand a squeeze and said, "Papa, it is Moshe!" She took off running toward him calling out, "Yes, Moshe! It is true! I've been made clean! I am whole again!"

The two young people came together in a fond embrace, tears streaming down both of their faces. Then Moshe pulled back and cradled Erstis' face with his hand. "Erstis, I have waited for you. I've never stopped loving you! I came as soon as I heard the news. I couldn't stay away!"

"I'm glad you came back early!" she gushed. "I didn't know how I was to wait another three days for your return."

"Now that you are whole, we can be wed!" He took a step back before he continued. "If you still want me, my love. Will you be my wife?"

"Oh, yes!" she cried. "I've never stopped loving you, either! I've dreamt of you often."

A broad smile came across Moshe's face. He pulled her close to him. She breathed in the scent of the oils he used on his sheep. He reverently placed his lips on her cheek. He licked the salty tears from his lips then gently kissed her other cheek, before pulling her close to him once more.

Erstis closed her eyes and sighed. *I'm healed! I'll be married to Moshe at last!*

"When my brother gets back from the hills with the herd," she said, "we are going to have a huge celebration. At that time, we can announce our marriage. I know Papa will agree!"

She turned to look at her Papa and saw him standing with his arm around her Mama. Their faces beamed as they watched the scene unfold before them. In her heart Erstis cried, *Oh thank you Yahweh! My prayers have been answered! You are our wonderful G-d! I love you and adore you! Thank you for answering my heart's prayer! This is even more wonderful than I could have imagined!*

The couple walked arm-in-arm toward the house, with smiles on their faces and sparkles in their eyes. Their minds were full of dreams for the future.

End Notes

1. A cor is a unit of measurement, equal to one homer or ten ephahs, equal to about eleven and one-ninth bushels (1 Kings 4:22, 5:11; 2 Chronicles 2:10, 27:5; Ezra 7:22).
2. "Te'enah" is the Hebrew word for both the fig-tree (*Ficus Carica*) and its fruit.
3. Psalm 121:1-2.
4. Song of Solomon 2:14.
5. "Yahweh" is a Hebrew name for G-d. It is believed to mean, "He brings into existence whatever exists."
6. Jehovah Rapha means "The Lord our healer."
7. Psalm 31:9-13a, 14, and 24.
8. "Shabbat" is the Hebrew word for Sabbath, and "Shalom" is the Hebrew word for Peace.
9. "Yeshua" is the Hebrew name for Jesus.
10. Psalm 7:1-5, 17.
11. "Abba" is a Syrian or Chaldean word for "Father", used to express warm affection, similar to the word "Daddy" today.
12. Malachi 4:2.
13. Jeremiah 31:34.
14. 2 Timothy 1:12
15. Psalm 48:1-2.
16. A "fortnight" is two weeks.

Coming Soon!

Did you enjoy Nameless ~A Story of Faith? Want more? Coming in 2018, is Nameless ~A Story of Courage. Meet Photina, the Samaritan woman that met Yeshua at Jacob's well. Although, the Bible doesn't record her name, the history books do. Her story is documented, and you can read it in my second book of the Nameless Trilogy.

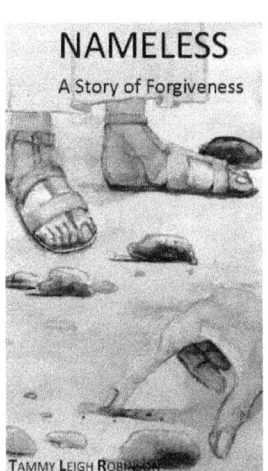

Can't get enough of angels, Hope and Faith? Walk with them through the pages of Nameless ~A Story of Forgiveness, as we meet the woman that was caught in adultery and brought to Yeshua. In the face of her sin, she deserved to be stoned to death. What led up to her choice to commit adultery? What dreams and goals did she have? Watch for the third book in 2020

About the author

Tammy Leigh Robinson is known as a daughter, mom, wife and friend. She is a survivor and now an author. Tammy survived the death of her six-month old daughter and the narrow escape from

 her own death after being taken hostage at gun point in Guatemala, as well as many other life experiences.

Although, she has faced many difficulties in life, Tammy continues to be goal oriented and work hard to reach her goals. Known for her optimism, Tammy focuses on helping others, encouraging them to reach for their goals and create WIN/WIN opportunities.

Tammy is a courageous businesswoman and for over ten years she has enjoyed speaking to women's groups, networking groups and the weekly Life Group that she hosts in her home.

As a mother of three grown children, Tammy states the most enjoyable season of her life was when she home schooled her children.

Nameless ~A Story of Faith is her first published book. This book represents many ideas and concepts. It is Tammy's dream come true as she has been writing since she started elementary school.

She counts herself fortunate to reside in the beautiful Niagara Region with her husband and soul mate, Keith Robinson. She's currently writing her second manuscript; Nameless ~A Story of Courage. She also has plans for the third book in her trilogy; Nameless ~A Story of Forgiveness.

www.ingramcontent.com/pod-product-compliance
Lightning Source LLC
Chambersburg PA
CBHW060115260626
47160CB00005B/1898